Tumbleweed Fever

By LJ Maas

D0888862

TUMBLEWEED FEVER
© 2009 BY LJ MAAS

ISBN 10: 1-933113-51-0
ISBN 13: 978-1-933113-51-7

First Published in 2000 by Yellow Rose Books.
First Intaglio Publications edition 2009

This Trade Paperback Is Published By
Intaglio Publications
Walker, LA USA
WWW.INTAGLIOPUB.COM

CREDITS
EXECUTIVE EDITOR: TARA YOUNG

COVER DESIGN BY SHERI

This book is dedicated to C.B. I believe LJ would have wanted it that way.

FOREWORD

LJ Maas passed away October 29, 2005, leaving behind a legion of fans and friends who were devastated by her untimely loss. Not only a gifted storyteller and author, LJ Maas was a gentle soul who left an indelible mark on everyone who knew her. No matter how much time passes, we will always feel the void that was created when she left this life.

Her spirit lives on in her writing, however, and we have done our best to preserve her voice while this book has undergone editing. If LJ were still with us, this book may have been edited differently, but without her input, we have chosen to keep things as they were originally written.

We must give special thanks to the one person who was affected more than anyone by LJ's passing—C.B., her partner. She has worked as diligently as anyone to bring LJ's work back into print. I think LJ would be extremely pleased with C.B.'s efforts.

We love you, C.B. Thank you for sharing this gift.

Sheri Payton and Kate Sweeney

Chapter One

The snow swirled around the wrangler, biting into any exposed flesh. The golden mare trudged on at its owner's insistence, the stable ahead of them only a shadow behind a curtain of white. The wrangler came to a stop in front of the barn, dismounting with weary effort. Pulling off rabbit skin mittens, the lone figure blew warm breath onto nearly frostbitten fingers, coaxing them into movement. Soon the digits could feel again, and a hand firmly grasped the latch, pulling the swinging door open.

Once inside, the howling bitter winds could be heard beating on the walls of the shelter, causing them to shake and creak. Leading the mare to an empty stall, the wrangler began to feel better as the heat from buckets of hot coals warmed the air. Stable hands tended to the buckets to keep the animals warm throughout the night. The saddle and blanket were pulled off the mare and hung over the stall rail to dry. Fatigued arms reached up and removed the saddlebags, carrying the few personal possessions the wrangler owned, including the precious notes. The wrangler laid the bags on the straw-strewn ground.

"There ya go, girl. Bet that feels better, huh, Alto?" a voice coarse with exhaustion said, while the wrangled used warm, dry pieces of burlap to massage the cold, tired muscles of the horse. After long minutes of a brush and currycomb, the horse nickered softly. Two large scoops of oats were placed in a feed bin in front of the horse and fresh hay tossed into the stall.

Picking up the saddlebags and pulling up the collar of a worn leather duster, the trail-weary soul pulled open the barn door and entered the bitter cold.

A world of white engulfed the wrangler. It did no good to look for landmarks. Even if it hadn't been the dead of night, there would be nothing to see but the driving snow. The wrangler backed up against the barn doors and carefully slid a tall muscular body along the length of the building. Nearing the corner of the barn, the wrangler held out an arm and wrapped a strong hand around a length of rope tied to the side of the stable.

A weathered Stetson fought off the full force of the icy blast, but wind and snow bit into the wrangler's face. Hand over hand, the wrangler followed the length of rope that led away from the barn. The snowdrifts had piled waist deep, and limbs that quickly became numb plodded on. The wrangler never gave in to the temptation to wipe the snow from frozen eyelashes; to let go of the rope was certain death. Experienced eyes had seen the bodies of men who had frozen to death not five feet from the door of their cabin because they had become lost in the all-encompassing whiteness.

Never losing touch with the lifeline that led to safety, the wrangler felt the wood of the bunkhouse, pushed hard against the door, and released the latch. Stepping inside the large wooden structure, the snow immediately began to melt, leaving a growing puddle on the floor.

The bunkhouse was the largest out-building on the ranch. Able to sleep forty men, it was nearly full as the new arrival pulled off dripping wet outer clothes. Two pot-bellied stoves burned warmly. One in the middle of the room held a coffeepot and an oversized pot that bubbled with some kind of stew. The second stove was near the door where the wrangler now stood removing a soaking wet duster, jacket, scarf, and mittens. Chairs were scattered around the smoking stove, draped with coats and blankets, to which the weary traveler added a few more articles of clothing.

A hearty laugh came from the back of the bunkhouse, and a giant of a man with long brown hair and soft brown eyes made his way across the room, stopping just in front of a grizzled-looking cowboy. The standing man held out his hand and the seated one slapped a few coins grudgingly into a waiting palm.

Turning toward the wrangler, the grizzled cowboy sneered. "You got more lives than a cat!" he spat out.

Another deep rumbling laugh came from the large man, his long strides quickly covering the distance between him and the wrangler. "Knew you'd make it, Dev. Can ya believe that iron-headed mutt bet against ya?"

The answer was a silent smirk; words would have taken more effort than the wrangler felt physically capable of now. The dark figure walked to the back of the room, toward a bunk set slightly apart from the others, and stopped short. Another cowboy lay sprawled across the bunk that had always been set apart for Devlin Brown.

"You're in my bunk," Devlin growled in a low, ominous voice.

"Go to hell," the cowboy returned, not bothering to open his eyes.

"You show me the way," Devlin hissed and grabbed the boy by his throat, nearly lifting him with one arm and flinging him to the floor.

The boy looked up at Devlin and at the double set of six guns hanging low on Devlin's hips. A mere tic of his eye telegraphed his intentions.

While the thought to move toward his holster was only a notion in his brain, Devlin's arm shot out and the boy swallowed hard. The movement was so fast it was a blur, and suddenly the boy was staring down the barrel of an ivory-handled pistol.

"If you're gonna think about it, you damn well better do it!" Devlin demanded, adding a touch of menace to the sound.

The boy lowered his gaze and muttered, "Sorry...didn't see nobody's name on it."

Devlin reached down and pulled a large bladed knife from a sheath wrapped around her lower leg. With a lightning fast movement, the blade of the Bowie knife sank into the wood at the top of the bunk. Devlin reached up and pulled the weathered Stetson from her head.

As soon as the hat came off, a long mane of raven hair tumbled down Devlin's back. She tossed off her short, inner leather jacket and threw it on top of the thin mattress. With the jacket removed, it was easy to see that the leather vest, which fit tightly against an old cotton shirt, and the pants that clung to sleek curves belonged to a woman. Hanging her hat over the handle of the still quivering knife, Devlin fixed an ice blue gaze down at the kneeling figure of the boy, his mouth hanging open at the sight above him.

"Devlin Brown! You see it now, boy?"

He had heard all the stories. Hadn't everyone? He knew immediately he was lucky to be alive.

"Yes, ma'am," he said in a trembling voice, rising and quickly gathering his belongings before moving to the other end of the bunkhouse, as far from Devlin's sight as he could manage.

Devlin watched the retreating figure of the young wrangler, more boy than man. She never intended to shoot him. The days when she would put a bullet through a man's heart just for looking at her in an odd manner were behind her, but not by much.

Hank's voice made her aware that she was still standing there motionless. Devlin moved to a table in the center of the room and sank into the offered chair. She wrapped her frozen fingers around a steaming mug of coffee. Hank placed a plate of stew and some cornbread in front of her and Devlin proceeded to devour the piping hot food.

"Slow down or you won't be able to taste it," Hank said with a chuckle.

"Don't matter what it tastes like," Devlin said, still shoveling in the food.

4

She was right, too. It never mattered. She'd eaten things to stay alive that would have made a billy goat puke, but she did as her friend suggested and slowed her pace. It had been three days since she'd had a hot meal and the food began to warm her belly. Once she took the time, she realized the meat was rabbit, her favorite. She found it hard to believe, but a person could get damn sick of eating beef every day. But on a cattle ranch, what else was there? Dried beef kept her alive on the range, but if she never saw another piece, she certainly wouldn't miss it.

Hank reached over and placed half of the coins he won on the table at her elbow. It seemed only right to share. It was because of Devlin that he'd won the bet anyway. She merely grunted and slid them into her pocket. Extra money meant a lot of whiskey or maybe a few shots of the good stuff. God, she loved the good stuff. Maybe even a night at Ellen's place.

Devlin felt herself smile slightly at the thought of a hot bath and a few hours in a soft bed and the even softer skin of one of the girls at Ellen's place. The smile quickly turned into a frown, however, when she remembered her last visit.

The young girl had been pretty enough and eager to please, but Devlin couldn't get that vision out of her mind. She had finally ended up paying Ellen for a hot bath and a good night's sleep before heading back to the ranch. The mental pictures began as soon as Devlin found the first note. Images of a mysterious woman, the one who had written the letter, filled Devlin's dreams at night.

Hank watched his friend as she ate. It had only been a short time before when Hank had decided to make it his mission to help reform the former outlaw. Two years previous, he'd joined up with a posse to help track down Devlin Brown's gang after they'd killed the husband and wife, owners of a ranch up in Pawnee, then brutally raped and murdered their young daughter. When the gang left, they rode off with fifty head of cattle, so they weren't too hard to track down.

Long before they caught up with the gang, the posse stopped to water their horses at a spring in some rock caverns. Hank saw the trail of blood and followed it into the cliffs. Stupid thing to do, he had said to himself, thinking it was probably a wounded mountain lion. What he found tucked into the crevice of rock was certainly as scary as any wounded cat.

Devlin had a couple of bullets in her shoulder, covered from head to toe in blood and bruises. She acted like a wounded animal, backing herself up against the rock and practically hissing at the man, her hand shaking weakly as she made a feeble attempt to lift her gun.

Hank knew that no matter what a person's past was, she could change if she really wanted to. His father had taught him that. He told Devlin that all it took was for her to take that first step. He stayed with the wounded woman, and much to her surprise, not only helped to get her on her feet again, but also never asked for anything in return. Devlin had grown accustomed to using her body to repay and cajole the men in her gang. So little by little, a bond of friendship formed between the two. It was later that Hank learned Devlin had been beaten, shot, and left for dead by her gang. Her crime had been attempting to stop the rape of the daughter of the ranch owners in Pawnee. Hank figured that meant that Devlin had already done the hard part, taking that first step.

Once Devlin had healed considerably, Hank vouched for her story when they met up with a U.S. Marshal from Kansas City. Hank even rode with Devlin for a year, chasing down some of the members of her gang. Her first temptation had been to shoot the men herself, but Hank had talked her into trying a different path. She deposited five men on the doorsteps of five different sheriffs' offices and courthouses over a large portion of the West. She saved up the money from the bounties she'd collected and sent it off to a sister of the rancher from Pawnee, who lived in St. Louis. It came to almost two thousand dollars. Hank dearly wished he could have been there when the woman opened that package.

Devlin slept soundly until the clock inside told her body it was near dawn. She rolled out of her bunk and rubbed her hands along her arms to get some warmth back into them. She stopped in front of the stove, opened the hinged door, and fed some wood into its belly, bringing it to life again. She then set the same pot of coffee over the metal plate on top of the stove.

She made her way easily in the dark, the light from the moon shining in through the gaps in the wood shutters and falling across the floor in little slices. She pulled the shutter open and peered out the window. The wind escaped through the frosty glass, pushing its way against her face. The snow had quit falling, but now they had the bitter wind with which to contend. As far as the eye could see, a blanket of bluish-white covered the plain. Its surface sparkled like diamonds. The temperature was falling fast, and the wind swirled the snow into drifts taller than Devlin stood.

Devlin sighed and dreamed once again of a winter that didn't mean spending days holed up in a cave or under an ice-soaked blanket on the open plain. She dreamed of a home where a fire and a good meal waited every night when she came in from the range. And always there was *her*, never a face, only a voice, and a feeling that this was the one. Devlin had always felt such desires, even though she would scarcely admit it to another living soul. Perhaps Hank, but that was because she knew he wouldn't laugh. He'd just tell her to go looking for her vision. The dreams hadn't started in earnest again until she had begun to find the notes. They were small squares of fancy writing parchment rolled up tightly and tied with cotton twine to a stray tumbleweed, which had been set loose on the prairie.

At first, she didn't know what to make of the tumbleweed with the note attached. It had blown quickly past and stuck to her blanket on the ground. It was hard not to miss the message, and something told Devlin that a woman had written it before she opened it. It just seemed like something a woman might do. When she looked at the delicate, precise handwriting, she could only read about half the words. Devlin had only gone to a proper school until she was eight. She tried to get along as best she could after that. She may not have been able to recognize all the words, but she felt the sentiment. The woman said she was tired of being alone, afraid of what the future would bring, and she wept for an aching heart that had never found true love.

Devlin turned from the window and went to pour two cups of coffee. Carrying them both, she walked to a bunk to the right of hers and set the tin cups on the floor. Flicking a wooden match with her thumbnail, the sliver of wood sparked to life. She inserted the match inside the kerosene lantern, which hung on the wall by the bunk, and turned the wick down low.

"Hank." She nudged Hank's huge body. Sprawled under the covers, his feet hung over the end of the mattress. "You up?"

"I reckon I am now," he said sleepily.

Devlin brought the lantern closer as Hank sat up and scratched his chest, leaning his head back to yawn. Devlin handed her drowsy friend a cup of coffee, and he mumbled his thanks.

Never having earned a reputation for good manners, Devlin unceremoniously shoved a piece of paper under her friend's nose. "What's this word?"

"Compromise," Hank sounded the word out for her. "It means, like you settle for something."

"How 'bout this one?" Dev pointed to another word on the paper.

"Solitary…means alone."

Devlin pulled perhaps a dozen sheets of paper from her vest pocket pointing to words she couldn't sound out or of which she had never learned the meaning. She never let Hank read the writing for himself. It was almost as though she was afraid to let anyone else touch the scraps of paper, as if that would make the dream disappear. He smiled at her when she wasn't looking, her brow furrowed in concentration as she wrote the meaning next to the word with writing lead she'd purchased from the general store.

Devlin squeezed her friend's shoulder in thanks and blew out the lantern. There was perhaps another hour of dark left. Everything was snowed in anyway, no sense in going out yet. She sat on her bunk, removing a bundle of the notes from her saddlebag and adding the new ones. She carefully looked around before she untied the ribbon that held the notes together. She knew it was a strange thing to carry around, and she didn't intend to take any grief over it.

She remembered seeing a woman tie up a bundle of letters from an old lover in a ribbon, and it seemed fitting for notes such as these. She remembered also her embarrassment at having to go into the general store, plunk down a penny on the counter, and ask for a length of ribbon. The worst part wasn't the way the shop girls looked at her and hoped she'd go away.

The worst part was having a girl ask her what color she wanted. That had thrown her. She hadn't thought about that part. She found herself saying "green." She didn't know why, but it seemed right somehow. When the girl held the ribbon up for Devlin's inspection, she smiled. That had put the shop girl at ease. Devlin didn't do it often, but when she did, the smile made her blue eyes sparkle. The store clerk had wrapped the deep green ribbon in a piece of paper, and Devlin carefully tucked it inside her shirt. Now every time Devlin fingered the silky ribbon, she thought of the mystery woman who haunted her dreams.

Devlin shook her head to remove the image from her mind. It didn't matter whether she was sleeping or awake. There was never a face. Devlin had kissed the lips a thousand times in her dreams but was never able to put a face to the vision. It had grown tougher every day to trudge through the mud, the rain, the snow, and the heat, all without a home to call her own.

She lay in her bunk, turning to face the wall. Hot tears stung her eyes, but she pushed them back. *No sense whimpering over what'll never be. God, it's gonna be a long winter.*

Sarah Tolliver leaned over and let more of the hot wax drip along the seam of the pine box. Peter had prepared her for this well, and she followed his instructions intently. He had built his own casket with what little strength he had left. He had been a carpenter, not a rancher, and it had been his last labor of love. He had warned Sarah that he would probably die during the harshest portion of the winter season, explaining how to seal the pine box, which would hold his body until the spring thaw made the ground warm enough to dig.

Tears slid down Sarah's face as she finished the tedious task. *Peter, please forgive me,* Sarah thought for the hundredth time in the past two months. She had cared for her husband until it seemed the inevitable was near. Sarah could no longer hold back the anguish that she had kept hidden for so many years. Peter would not rest until his wife had admitted the truth to him.

Sarah sobbed when she asked Peter to forgive her. She had never meant to hurt him, but the truth was that it was *her* dream to come west. It had been *her* dream to be a rancher, not his. He had been a carpenter with a gentle soul and a giving nature. He just didn't have the mental toughness and grit it took to live life in the Oklahoma Territory.

As illness ravaged his body, Sarah confessed that although she would always hold a place in her heart for the father of their two children, she had never loved Peter the way his wife should have loved him. She had cared for him and stood by him, but the passion and love had never developed for a man who would always remain more friend than lover.

"Sarah...Sarah," Peter whispered. "Little one, don't you think I know this? There was nothing more important to you than leaving Kentucky and being independent, I know that. I married you knowing that I would always be second best in your heart."

Peter forced a weak smile. He stroked the face surrounded by hair the color of honey, looking into eyes that were a deep emerald green.

"Sarah, this has always been enough for me and I've never regretted my life with you, not once. You gave me a strong son and a beautiful daughter. You've been my strength through all our years together. Please don't cry." He brushed her tears aside.

Peter pulled Sarah toward him and kissed her forehead. "You could never have loved me that way. I guess I knew that your heart was always meant for someone else. Sarah…" he said sharply until the young woman looked into his soft gray eyes. "You're still a young woman. Please don't make the same mistake again."

Peter squeezed Sarah's hand tightly, knowing the words he spoke would be his last.

"Sarah…next time…don't settle for less than your heart's desire."

The snow was deep and the wind bitter when the sun rose the next morning, but with the help of a litter, her son, and Atlas, a large black gelding, Sarah placed Peter's casket in the root cellar, sealed with wax and wrapped in burlap sacks. Before she took the body from the barn, she and the children stood by the pine box and said their goodbyes. She watched her children as they gently touched the box where their father lay. Matthew, at eleven, tried hard not to cry, taking his new role as man of the house seriously. Hannah was only six. With strawberry blond hair and green eyes the color of her mother's, Hannah looked angelic. Sarah read a poem that had been one of Peter's favorites, then she settled Hannah back inside the cabin before moving Peter's remains.

Once inside the warmth of the cabin, Sarah looked around and began thinking of all the things that were now her responsibility. Peter may not have fancied himself much of a cattleman, but they had one of the most prosperous ranches around for its size, aside from Sarah's uncle's. Sarah learned two things from her father before he died at Gettysburg. He had taught her about horses and cattle. She now realized that her knowledge of both would be put to the test.

Sarah pulled out pieces of Matthew's clothing from a chest, which rested next to the ladder up to the loft. Holding up the pants, she realized her son was as tall as she was.

"Mom, what are you doing?" the boy asked.

"We need to get some feed out to the cattle up on the north ridge. Actually, I think we should bring them down to the pasture and fence them in. We have plenty of hay and grain to last till the snow thaws, but we need to take care of this place. You can't do it alone, and I certainly can't do it in a dress."

The wind was bitter, but Sarah brought a large log onto the porch and set it on its end. Then bundling up Hannah, she showed the girl how to climb onto the log and clang the metal alarm should there be an emergency while Sarah and Matt were outside.

The sun sank behind the white crested mountains in the distance before mother and son returned from their work. Sarah stripped off her freezing wet clothes and wrapped a blanket around her before starting a fire in the stone fireplace. She warmed herself and pulled on dry clothes, going into the main part of the cabin and checking on the stew she'd put over a low part of the fire earlier in the day.

After supper, Hannah fell asleep quickly, while Matthew watched the flames dance in the fireplace. Sarah pulled out pen and paper and made long lists of chores, things that were now new to her.

"What are ya doin', Mom?" Matthew asked.

"Mostly trying to organize my thoughts. It's going to be quite a job keeping everything going until spring. Once the thaw comes, we can get some help from Uncle Art. With the size of the herd, we may have to hire wranglers come the warm weather."

Sarah didn't want to frighten the boy, but winter was a

time when the only thing that took a herd was death. Once spring arrived, that would change. Rustlers and thieves would soon hear that the Double Deuce ranch was without a man's protection, and her herd would begin to disappear. She would be lucky indeed if they stopped at her cattle, and a shiver ran through her body. She wasn't much with a pistol, although her father had taught her to shoot a rifle. Her skill with a Winchester eventually bested his. Yes, wranglers and guns meant power, and in the Oklahoma Territory, she needed both to survive.

"Go on to bed, Matt, it's late," she said, still lost in thought.

Once Sarah was alone, she pulled her small journal open and wrote her thoughts onto a small square of parchment. It had been almost a year since she had started placing her innermost thoughts and desires down on paper. It made it easier somehow, easier to face each day with the realization that she would never have what she dreamed of. Sarah wasn't naïve enough to think a lover would solve all her problems, but she longed for someone to complete her—the other half of her soul.

Tucking the tightly rolled parchment into her apron pocket, she carefully banked the fire and went to bed. Lying in the large bed alone only served to increase her feelings of loneliness. She closed her eyes and let the vision of her soul mate wash over her. She didn't know what the other half of her soul would look like, but she didn't care. It was a sensation, an emotion that stirred her more than a physical body. Strong arms that would hold her through the night and make her feel loved and protected. Someone who would understand who she was and what she wanted out of life just by knowing her.

Turning to lie on her side, she let the tears slide across her cheeks. She cried silently for what she realized would never be.

So why do I keep hoping? God, it's going to be a long winter.

Chapter Two

Arthur Winston looked at the small group in front of him. Good trail bosses, but a motley group to be taking to a barbecue. Out of the whole bunch, he figured the only one who would be able to act like a gentleman in a social situation would be Hank. Then again, the only woman there would be his niece, and any man here would be a fool to try anything with his employer's niece. Well, the only woman if he didn't count Dev, and Art didn't. Besides, this barbecue wasn't exactly a social call.

There would be four other cattlemen there, each having his trail bosses in tow. The wranglers became a sort of status symbol in the territory. The more wranglers you could afford to hire, the wealthier a rancher you were—simple concept. Art didn't have as many as some, but he still ran one of the biggest ranches this side of the Mississippi. He didn't need as many wranglers; he hired the best there was. They were good cowpunchers, full of grit and determination. Most of them were just this side of the law, but when a rancher paid good wages, the wranglers rode for the brand.

"I know it isn't Saturday, but take a bath anyway, we got a barbecue to go to tomorrow" was all he said, knowing they would follow his orders without question.

When the wranglers turned to go, grumbling a little, Art turned toward Devlin.

"Dev, got a minute?" he asked, indicating she should follow him into the house.

Devlin nodded and followed. She liked this old man who

was tough as nails on the outside but as fair as the day was long. He was a true cattleman. He never put up barbed wire fences, just let his steers share pasture with the few buffalo left, leaving it up to his wranglers to keep a rein on the herds. Devlin had a problem with men putting up fences to show they owned the land. The Choctaw had taught her that it was impossible to own something as great as the earth under your feet. White men just didn't get that.

"Sit down, Dev." Art motioned to a chair across from the large wooden desk in the study.

Devlin sat back into the leather-covered chair; the softness of the cushions felt good on her stiff back. Her shoulders had started giving her problems more and more lately, probably from old bullet wounds. Art offered her a smoke, which she refused, and a glass of whiskey, which she hurriedly accepted. Feeling the smooth liquor slide down her throat, she smiled.

Art smiled at the woman, her head tilted back slightly, eyes half closed as she savored the first sip of the amber liquid. He'd never known a woman who enjoyed a good whiskey like she did. Well, maybe there was one other.

"Got a proposition for you, Dev," Art said, interrupting the silence.

Devlin's eyebrow arched, waiting for his next words.

"I want to offer you a deal to go over and work at my niece's ranch, the Double Deuce."

Devlin smiled at the joke, then realized Art was serious. She downed the rest of her drink in one gulp and stood to leave.

"You want me to work for a woman? Forget it," she said loudly.

"Come on, at least let's talk about it. The money will be good. I can promise you that—"

"There isn't that much money in the whole world!" she countered, but she did sit back down.

Art poured them another drink and left the bottle in front of Devlin.

"She's got a nice small ranch about twenty-five miles south

of here. Her husband died over the winter, and she'll lose the place if she can't get a wrangler there to protect her interests. I can't find anybody I trust enough who would be willing to take the job. This barbecue we're going to tomorrow may just be the end unless I can hire somebody for her. All the big men will be there, and John Montgomery is none too pleased that she decided to stay on and run the place after her husband died."

Dev lifted her hat and ran her hands through her hair, looking uncomfortable. *John Montgomery...what a spineless bastard. Walks around in a dude's suit actin' like he owns the territory. Doesn't even wear a gun.* To Dev, that only meant one thing. He hired out his killing.

"Why don't ya just bring her here? You got a big place. She'll be safe and sound, no worries."

Art gave Devlin a crooked smile.

"You haven't met my niece. She's not exactly the kind of woman who likes being taken care of. That damn ranch is her whole life." He wiped his face with a large calloused hand.

"Dev, I know about your past...hell, every kid that can read a dime novel knows about Devlin Brown, but I want you to know you're one of the few I'd trust my niece's care to. I wasn't just blowin' smoke when I said I'd make the offer worth it, either. You don't want to spend the rest of your life as a wrangler, do you?"

Devlin thought about that. In the past, she had only thought about her day-to-day existence. Now she could actually think about tomorrow and the day after that. Didn't she feel it herself, the feeling that just scratching out an existence wasn't enough anymore?

"You take the job over at the Double Deuce and I'll see it you get top wages. You stay for two years and I'll set you up with a starter herd myself. I'll let you cut out twenty-five head of my best stock...even throw in some acreage if you feel like settlin' down here." Art waited for Devlin's answer.

Devlin couldn't make herself do it—work for a woman. Frankly, the more she thought about it, the worse it sounded, but that wasn't the real reason and she knew it. Devlin said the words aloud to convince herself, but she couldn't hide from her thoughts. There was only one reason in turning down an offer so good. People like Devlin Brown didn't deserve chances like this. She had too much to make up for, too many past misdeeds to repay. Being a wrangler with no hope of a future, no chance at love and a family, that was Devlin Brown's penance, and she couldn't give in to the hope that there might be something more waiting for her.

"Sorry, Mr. Winston, but I just can't, it just wouldn't work out. Just move her here and tell her that's the way it's gonna be. Best thing all around."

Art smiled sadly and shook Devlin's hand. "Like I said, you've never met Sarah."

The next day, Arthur Winston walked alongside the corral with his niece, who in turn watched her son turn a spit that held the side of beef that would be the main course. "How are you really doing, Sarah?"

"Some days are better than others." She smiled warmly back at her uncle.

"Look, I know you want to stay here, and if an old man's opinion means anything at all, you're doing a great job. I'm proud of you. I have to tell you, though, playing the hostess and charming the pants off these men here today won't stop what they want." He needed to be honest with her.

"I think deep down I know that, too, Uncle Art, but I have to try everything." Sarah leaned on a rail and looked at the mounts moving around in the corral. "I won't give up, no matter what they decide." She laid her forehead onto her arm in a weary fashion.

The sound of galloping horses drew their attention. Two riders came in and quickly dismounted—a large man with smiling brown eyes and a female figure, who caused Sarah's eyes to widen.

Dust and grime from the trail covered Devlin. She had meant to stay away from the gathering; that many people in one place made her nervous, but Mr. Winston was the boss. He had sent Hank after the prodigal wrangler, and Devlin's friend caught up with her, trying to pull a spring calf out of a shallow ravine.

"Sarah, here's an example of two of the best," Art said, slipping a protective arm around his niece's waist. "Hank Sutton, this is my niece, Mrs. Sarah Tolliver."

Hank stepped forward and gently took the offered hand. "Very nice to meet you, Mrs. Tolliver. Nice spread you got here. Awful glad you invited us, thanks."

Sarah immediately liked the man who towered over her small frame. He had a kind face and she enjoyed the way his eyes smiled before he did. As she shook his hand, however, out of the corner of her eye, she watched Devlin standing next to him. Sarah felt the intensity of the other woman's gaze, and her body felt somewhat exposed under the scrutiny.

"This is Devlin Brown," her uncle introduced the dirty wrangler.

"Oh," Sarah said.

Devlin lifted her head, her eyes no longer hidden under the shadow of the brim of her hat. Devlin fully expected to see fear in the young woman's eyes, especially after her startled gasp. When she looked at Sarah, Devlin didn't see fear at all. She thought it looked a lot like…amusement.

Devlin realized the woman held her hand out. Devlin gazed down at the dirty leather gloves she wore. Pulling one off with her teeth, she wiped her mud-streaked, sweaty hand on her pants, only making matters worse. Devlin wasn't used to such social situations, not with a real lady, anyway. The only kind of women she had any experience with were the ones she touched for a price. They never cared how dirty she was. Not knowing what else to do, Devlin shrugged as if to apologize. Her expression seemed to say that she wouldn't be offended if Sarah didn't accept her dirty hand.

Sarah took a step closer and firmly took Devlin's hand, gently squeezing the calloused fingers and ignoring the red dirt. Devlin thought she had never felt anything as warm and reassuring as the young woman's handshake.

"There's a rain barrel around back by the wood pile, get yourself cleaned up. You two are sitting at the main table with me," Art said. Each of the cattlemen sat two of his best wranglers at the table with them.

Devlin turned and headed for the back of the house as Sarah watched her movements.

Sarah brought out a bar of soap for Devlin, who stammered her thanks and sniffed at the soap, smiling to herself at the flowery scent. She removed a weathered red bandanna from her neck along with her filthy shirt, exposing a woolen undershirt, once white but now gray and tattered. Devlin soaked her hair and washed her face and neck in the cool water, all the while watching a tiny figure out of the corner of her eye. Devlin flipped her hair back and stared down at the little girl, who stared back intently. Finally, a shy smile appeared on the girl's face and Devlin couldn't resist.

Kneeling down, she wiped the dripping water from her eyes and whispered at the girl, "Boo!"

Hannah squealed, and the giggling girl ran right into her mother's legs as Sarah came around the corner.

"Hannah." Sarah couldn't help smiling. "Don't bother Miss Brown."

Devlin thought her ears were playing tricks on her. Only in her dreams had she ever heard a woman's voice so captivating. It was smooth and slid slowly across her senses like honey.

"She's not a bother, ma'am," Devlin said, straightening up to tower over Sarah.

Sarah couldn't speak and almost forgot why she'd come back outside. Devlin seemed to be able to say so much with only a look, and Sarah didn't quite understand the heat that rose to her cheeks.

"I…um…I forgot to bring you a towel," Sarah said, holding out the soft cloth.

The silence lingered until Devlin fingered her woolen undergarment.

"Sorry, I don't have a clean shirt. I hope that doesn't bother you."

Sarah looked up from her daughter's tugging on her skirt into the apologetic gaze. "I think we can fix that. Follow me." Sarah paused to judge the width of Devlin's shoulders and walked off.

Devlin watched the retreating figure and bristled at the command. She wasn't used to having a woman order her around, but she didn't want to offend her boss's niece. Looking around to see if anyone was watching, Devlin shrugged to a smiling Hannah, who still stood by the woodpile, and trotted off to follow Sarah as she entered the barn.

Sarah opened a small storeroom and knelt in front of an open chest. She selected a dark gray shirt and as an afterthought pulled out a button-up, cotton undershirt. She stood, closing the chest and handed the neatly folded clothes to Devlin.

Devlin fingered the cloth tentatively, uncertain what she should do. The last thing she needed was charity. "Thanks, but I can't." She tried to hand them back.

Sarah could see the pride warring against the sensibility within Devlin. It appeared as though kindness was something foreign to her. "Take them or not, Miss Brown, it's certainly your choice." Sarah turned to leave the barn. "My son is eleven, but the moths will have these long before he'll be big enough to fit into them."

Sarah left the barn and Dev stood holding the clothes, unsure of what had just transpired. She knew one thing, however. She wanted to hear more of that woman's lovely voice. Listening to her body instead of reason, Devlin quickly stripped, pulling on the crisp, clean clothes.

Having hastily finished dressing, Devlin walked through the open door and made her way to the table where Hank and

Mr. Winston already sat. Hank's jaw nearly hit the table. He had never seen Devlin look so…he hardly had words for it. She had scrubbed her face clean and combed her hair back, fixing it into a single braid down her back. She wore a dark gray shirt under her usual black leather vest that she left open instead of buckled up the front.

Sarah had just placed two large platters of biscuits on the table, looking up as Devlin came inside. Their eyes met and held in a frank gaze.

Devlin felt the brim of her hat still on her head. Quickly pulling it off, she noticed all eyes on her.

"Ma'am," she said in a low voice as she pulled the Stetson from her head.

Sarah smiled at Devlin wearing the clean clothes. "Miss Brown," she acknowledged and sat at the head of the table near her uncle.

Hank saw the brief, unspoken exchange between his friend and their beautiful young hostess. He grinned into his plate, wondering if either of them were aware of it yet, stunned at how hard and fast his friend just fell.

The food was the best any man was likely to taste for a long time. Sarah spared no expense and attempted for the rest of the afternoon and evening to keep the men entertained and happy. After the men outside had eaten, they tapped a keg of beer. The sound of laughing and loud talk filtered up to the cabin.

Sarah heard Matthew's fiddle, and she worried about how he fared with the wranglers.

Inside the cabin, Sarah and the cattlemen finally arrived at the reason for the party. The men and their wranglers took a short break to stretch their legs. They started to filter back into the large room when Sarah's uncle pulled her aside. Waiting until he thought everyone had entered the cabin, he spoke quietly.

"Sarah, you can't come inside, not unless they ask for you." He wasn't able to meet Sarah's gaze.

"A meeting about me…how *they're* going to dispose of *my* life, and I can't come in? Because I'm a woman?" The temper she had inherited from her father rose swiftly.

"They're set in their ways. Not much I can do about it, darlin'. Sarah…I couldn't find anyone willing to ride for your brand," Art said, knowing what it meant to her.

"You don't have to go back east. You and the children will always have a home with me," Art continued, knowing Sarah only heard half of what he said. "In fact, you'll be a wealthy young woman. They intend to give you a generous price for the land and your stock. Maybe you could start thinking about looking for a man. I mean, if you had a husband, they wouldn't be able to drive you out this way."

Sarah felt tears threatening. "I did that once. I won't do it again. If I have to lose everything I have and die alone, the next time I marry, it will only be for love."

She turned her back to him, and he recognized the proud body language as one of his own family traits. He quietly went inside to wait for the others to return and start the meeting.

Devlin stood in the shadows of the cabin as the young woman and her uncle spoke. She hadn't meant to eavesdrop, but by the time she realized they were carrying on a private conversation, it was too late to speak up without embarrassing someone.

Devlin watched as Sarah's shoulders slumped in defeat. She wouldn't let anyone see it, but once Sarah was alone, she became just a young woman trying to carry more of a burden than should have been her fair share. Devlin had listened throughout the day to the stories the other wranglers had told about the winter the woman had to endure, how just about everything around them had been her doing. Now she was about to have it taken away because she didn't wear pants and a pair of six guns.

Devlin cleared her throat and pretended she had just walked up to the cabin. Sarah turned and caught a glimpse of her. Sarah stood there expectantly as if waiting for Devlin to speak.

"Nice place you got here," Devlin said weakly, unable to come up with any sort of small talk.

"Hurry into the meeting, you'll be able to buy it cheap," she said bitterly.

Seeing the surprise on Devlin's face, Sarah hurried to apologize. "God, I'm sorry! I have no right to take this out on you. I apologize for my rudeness."

The corners of Devlin's mouth turned upward. "You're plenty mad. Don't apologize for tellin' the truth."

Sarah's head lowered for a moment. She turned her face into the warm evening breeze and closed her eyes. Tears threatened once more, but she swore she wouldn't cry. She told herself she wouldn't give the men the satisfaction of seeing her weep.

"I think I'll miss the cedar trees the most. The way they stand so strong, yet bend almost to the ground during a wind storm," Sarah said dreamily.

"To bend but never break," Devlin found herself saying.

Sarah turned and looked at Devlin, not quite understanding her body's overwhelming desire to have this mysterious woman hold her in strong arms. Devlin looked deep into the jade-colored eyes, watching with slight amusement as a light flush colored the young woman's cheeks. There was such sadness about her, and Devlin thought about the reason. What if everything she had worked her whole life for was about to be stolen by John Montgomery and his idiot friends?

"Well, here I go…bending but not about to let them see me break." Sarah walked into the cabin followed by a thoughtful Devlin.

Sarah bustled around the table like a good hostess. She caught Devlin's eye and Devlin grinned back conspiratorially at Sarah's Southern belle routine. She opened a large wooden box and offered each man a cigar, even stopping to light her uncle's with a brand from the fire.

Art looked at his niece and wondered if the strain had finally driven her *loco*. She acted like the belle she'd never really been, jumping up to bring cigars and coffee to the seated guests. He eyed her suspiciously, nearly afraid to drink the coffee she'd brought him after she leaned over and gave him a flame for his cigar.

Sarah pulled a bottle of liquor from a cabinet and poured each of them—including herself, to Devlin's amusement—a shot from the bottle. She held her cup aloft and tipped it slightly to the group.

"Gentlemen...Miss Brown...to the future."

A couple of them nearly spit their drinks out in surprise. Most of them just looked damned uncomfortable. Sarah, not missing a beat, swallowed the amber liquid in one gulp, a satisfied smirk on her face.

None of the woman's actions was lost on Dev, even as she enjoyed her own drink. *Good God, she's got the face of an angel and the temper of a whore. It musta killed her old man just trying to keep up with her!*

Devlin had experienced top-of-the-line liquor in a number of fine establishments, but this had to be the finest whiskey that had ever slid across her tongue. Her satisfaction showed in her face.

"You enjoy a good Kentucky bourbon, Miss Brown?" Sarah asked.

Devlin answered with a large toothy grin, the smile that she rarely used. "Never before, ma'am, but I gotta say, it's my drink of choice from here on in."

Sarah leaned her back head and laughed. It was genuine, and it felt good to be able to regain a small piece of her sense of humor, if only for a moment.

"Well, I'll leave you to your discussions then," she said. Squeezing her uncle's hand, she looked into blue eyes taking her in. Sarah smiled and left the cabin with as much grace and dignity as a queen.

Devlin was thunderstruck. She had been from the moment the woman's lilting laugh filled up her senses.

Then Sarah had smiled at Devlin.

Devlin's legs involuntarily parted wider under the table as she felt an incredible heat radiate up her body from her aching center. Devlin knew right then she would do anything to see that smile, hear that laughter directed at her, including ride for the brand of the Double Deuce, ride for a woman.

No, no, no! What the hell are you thinking? Damn, you're letting what's between your legs do your thinking for you! Okay, she's beautiful, and she may be a spitfire, but she is a lady, not a whore. There is no way on this earth that woman is ever gonna let you touch her, so what the hell are you dreaming about?

"That little girl sets a mighty fine table," Montgomery said.

By this time, Devlin's blood boiled. She wanted to hit someone, and it took every meditative technique she knew not to follow through with that feeling. She ran a hand over her face and took a deep breath.

"Mr. Winston," she whispered, leaning toward the man on her right. "I changed my mind."

Sarah watched as the door to her cabin opened and a line of men with grim faces walked out. The outward dispositions changed once she saw her uncle and Hank. They wore ear-to-ear grins.

"Thank you for a wonderful day, Mrs. Tolliver. It was… um…" John Montgomery cast an uneasy eye toward Devlin. "It was…educational."

One by one, the men shook Sarah's hand and thanked her before leaving.

"You've been reprieved, darlin,'" her uncle said. "Meet your new wrangler."

Sarah looked into Hank's face, the sly grin still in place. Art nudged Devlin in the back to push her forward a step or two, and she finally raised her head. She appeared to blush as she touched the brim of her hat.

"Ma'am" was the only word Devlin uttered.

The look of surprise on Sarah's face was evident, but her happiness soon overpowered it. She smiled at Devlin again, causing the blush on Devlin's face to deepen.

"Thank you, Miss Brown," Sarah said.

"Yes, ma'am."

Sarah spent a few moments talking alone to her uncle and watched as he rode toward home. The other wranglers, some having let the beer get to them a little, milled around and mounted up while Devlin moved her saddlebags into the barn. She returned to where the other wranglers stood, arms folded, making sure they all got on their way, already taking her job seriously. She had promised Mr. Winston that she would not only ride, but also keep an eye out for his niece and her children.

Sarah said good night and easily fought off each unwelcome advance as though she had years of experience doing that. When she turned back toward her cabin, she heard the slurred voice of the wrangler she just turned down.

"Dev? Out here? Kind of like puttin' the fox in charge of the henhouse!"

From out of the shadows, Devlin tapped the big man on the shoulder. When he turned, she had her arm cocked and ready. Her right arm shot forward, her fist landing in the middle of the drunken mans face. He looked stunned for a full second until his knees finally got the message from his alcohol-clouded brain and crumpled under him.

The other wranglers laughed at their fallen comrade. Devlin walked past Sarah, who had witnessed the exchange with some amusement. Devlin scooped up a bucket of water from the trough and unceremoniously dumped it on the unconscious wrangler.

Shaking their heads and laughing, the other men threw their saddle mate over his horse and rode off.

Sarah looked up at Devlin, catching her gaze. Sarah suddenly felt shy and awkward around her.

"Do you need to get your things? I mean, did you want to

start tomorrow?" Sarah asked.

"Have all I need with me, Mrs. Tolliver. I'll just bed down in the barn and—"

"Oh, no. I mean, we have a room around back. It's not as big as a bunkhouse, but then again, I never thought I'd be hiring a wrangler."

"I think we ought to get something straight right off, Mrs. Tolliver. I work for your uncle. I'd really prefer it if you weren't to tell folks *you* hired me." Devlin looked Sarah in the eye, her gaze narrowing.

Sarah opened her mouth to speak and promptly closed it again. *All right, calm down...you need this woman.* "I guess I'm a little surprised at that remark. You have trouble working for a woman? Who do you think is paying your wage, Miss Brown? You may get it from my uncle's hand, but by God, it will come from my bank account! I thought you felt differently. You *are* a woman, are you not?"

That last bit was probably pushing it, but Sarah had quite a temper once she got going. Problem was, she had a hard time reining it in once she let go. Sarah realized she had crossed a line when Devlin's gaze lifted, her eyebrow arching in a combination of intimidation and seduction. Devlin took a step forward, closing the distance until there were a few inches between them. Devlin's height made her an even more imposing figure.

Her normally blue gaze turning pale as ice, Devlin's voice lowered until the words came out as a growl. "I *am* a woman, Mrs. Tolliver. A woman who doesn't think twice about killin' a man in a fair fight nor takin' a grown woman that's actin' like a child over my knee. So if you want me as a wrangler on this spread, let's just pretend and say I work for your uncle, shall we?"

If Devlin hadn't been so mad, she would have laughed aloud at the expression on Sarah's face. Sarah appeared as though she didn't know if she should be terrified, slap Devlin's face, or spit in her eye. She chose none of the above and abruptly turned on her heel and stomped off into the house.

Before Devlin could move, Sarah was back and threw a bundle of blankets at Devlin's chest. She held a lantern and moved toward the back of the house.

"Follow me." She stopped and took a deep breath. "Please."

Devlin smirked at the woman's back, enjoying the return of her customary control. She had been feeling like a fish out of water, stammering and stuttering like a lovesick schoolboy. This woman with the emerald eyes was a prize, no doubt, but it was about time she saw the real Devlin and found out she wasn't one to be ordered about like a field hand.

Devlin looked around the inside of the room. It could have slept four men easily. She hadn't had a room to call her own since she was an outlaw. Then she'd stayed in fancy hotels and put her men up in the local brothels. She remembered seeing cantinas in old Mexico smaller than this.

In the meantime, Sarah's temper had begun to cool some. She quickly realized that she wasn't going to be able to run roughshod over this wrangler. Devlin wouldn't be intimidated by Sarah's sharp tongue or charmed into coercion by a few batting eyelashes. Sarah had spent so much time dealing with men; she'd nearly forgotten that she didn't have to deal with another woman. Honesty brought about better results.

"Miss Brown?"

"Yes, Mrs. Tolliver?"

"Why did you hit that man? Was it because of what he said?"

"I don't much care about what people say about me. I've heard it all. It just riled me when I figured…well, you know, there's such a thing as a lady's honor…" She trailed off. *How is it that this gal can make me trip over my tongue just by looking at me?*

Devlin ran an appraising look up and down the woman's small frame. "Don't tell me you never had anybody fight over ya before?" she said with a slight grin.

Sarah looked into Devlin's electric gaze. "Over me, yes. For me...never."

It seemed to the two women that a long time passed as they stood toe to toe looking at each other, but in reality, only seconds had gone by. Devlin was the first to break away, moving to open the door to her new room.

"I better go do a ride-through to check up on the herd. You wanna give me the lay of the land?"

"I'll go with you."

"That's why you have me, ma'am. It's my job now."

"But in the dark? Won't that be dangerous if you don't know where you're going?"

Devlin raised an eyebrow and fixed a perturbed glance at the woman until Sarah gave her the necessary information. Once Devlin saddled Alto again, Sarah came out to talk with Devlin.

"Are you sure I shouldn't draw you a map or something? How will you be able to get around?"

"You'll just have to trust me, Mrs. Tolliver," Devlin said, lowering her voice an octave and pulling her hat snugly on her head.

The look Devlin leveled at Sarah as she reined her horse's neck to turn the animal sent a thunderbolt-like jolt right through Sarah's body. The heat of that impact focused itself right between her legs.

Devlin didn't have to ride far. The Tollivers had pastured most of the herd on the north ridge, an area close to the family's cabin. Devlin returned rather quickly, pushing open the door to the room near the back of the house that she now called her own. Lighting the lamp on a small wooden table by the bed, she saw a small chest lying on the floor near the end of the bunk. Devlin recognized it as the same chest Sarah had gone through in the barn when she had given Devlin clean clothes. Kneeling down and lifting the lid, she saw shirts and assorted pieces of clothing. On top of the clothing lay an unopened bottle of Kentucky bourbon. Devlin didn't know whether to throw the stuff back in the woman's face or take her in her arms and never let go.

She picked up the bottle, tossed her hat on the chair, and pulled two notes from her pocket. Opening the bottle, she took a long swallow. The smooth liquid slid easily down her throat, infusing her belly with its warmth. Leaning her long frame back on the bunk, she held the paper up to the light. Devlin was surprised to find two notes that far south. Doing her best, she slowly read the words aloud.

There is only the night sky to talk to...no one else to share my smiles and my tears.
Just like the fairy tales I used to read, my head is filled with thoughts of a dark warrior riding a pale horse.
One day, the warrior rides over the ridge and carries me off, and I am safe in strong arms.
I will wait for forever this time...waiting for the dark warrior...

She reached out and gently brushed her fingers across the worn and dirty parchment, her hand crossing a discolored spot that looked as if the ink had been blurred by a single teardrop. She unrolled the next note and read, and even though she couldn't understand why, her hands shook slightly as they held the parchment.

No one has ever held my heart, not the way that I dream of...
Is it wrong to wish for a lover that will captivate my heart, as well as my body?
Too long have I waited for the warrior of my soul...I am thinking that I will always be alone,
All that my heart desires is right here, all around me, everywhere I look,
Still it means so little without someone to share it.

Devlin pulled off her spurs and kicked off her boots, rolling over to let a warm puff of breath blow out the lamp. Her body was tired, and her eyes ached for sleep, yet it was a long time in coming.

When she finally relaxed her mind enough for sleep to claim her, the mysterious woman haunted her dreams, only this time, she had long hair the color of wheat and smiling emerald eyes.

Chapter Three

Dawn was still an hour away when Sarah pulled herself from her warm bed the next morning. Feeling bone tired, she wished she had no chores or obligations, no one to fend for but herself. On such a day, she swore that if she had the choice, she would pull the covers over her head and stay in bed until the sun was high in the sky. Unfortunately, she had mouths to feed and a ranch to run.

"That is, if Devlin Brown lets me," she said aloud, feeling guilty at her flair of temper.

She washed her face and brushed her hair, pulling it back into a braid. She knew that she had acted like a petulant child the night before and hoped Devlin had accepted the bottle of her father's best as a peace offering.

Sarah had sat up into the night reading until she heard Devlin's horse enter the corral. Surprisingly, she fell asleep rather quickly after that. It was due to the odd feeling that everything didn't hang on her own shoulders. Someone watched over for her for a change. At first, she bristled at the thought that she might need looking after.

For some reason, Sarah remembered the fire in Devlin's angry eyes when she had stepped in close to Sarah and again, the possessive look in Devlin's eye right before she laid the drunken man out with one punch. Sarah didn't want to admit it, not even to herself, but deep down, she enjoyed the notion of having a protector.

Devlin paused, her saddle thrown over one shoulder and Alto's blanket in hand when the door to the cabin opened. The sun had just peeked over the ridge, the valley still in the shadows of night. Sarah walked toward Devlin, wiping her hands on a small towel. It seemed as if neither woman knew what to say to the other.

"You'll at least eat meals with us, Miss Brown?" Sarah asked awkwardly.

Devlin took one whiff of the tempting aroma coming from the house, and her stomach rumbled. She raised her head and grinned. "Yes, ma'am."

As they walked through the door to the cabin, both women breathed a soundless sigh of relief at the truce that had formed between them.

Devlin admitted to herself that she hadn't tasted food so good since she had stayed at a hotel in Kansas City. Steak, eggs, and biscuits and gravy. If she ate one more bite, Alto would be giving her dirty looks. Dev sipped her coffee while sneaking looks at Sarah, who talked and good-naturedly teased her children.

Devlin wasn't much for small talk, and at first, Sarah's chatter made her nervous, but now, sitting there watching the family's interaction, Sarah's voice and easy laughter acted as a balm to Devlin's characteristic edginess.

"What will you do today, Miss Brown?" Sarah looked across the table at Devlin.

"You got cows ready to calf. I put 'em in the pastureland at the bottom of the hill. Need to make sure no wolves or big cats show up. They'll stay away if they see humans around 'em, though." Devlin took another swallow of her coffee. "Might need some help today. You up for it, boy?" She nodded in Matthew's direction.

Matt's eyes lit up and he turned to his mother. "Can I, Mom?"

"May I."

"Sorry. May I?"

"Of course you may as long as you do everything Miss Brown tells you." Sarah then addressed Devlin. "You will watch out for him, won't you?"

Devlin swallowed the remainder of her coffee, reaching over to tousle the boy's hair. "Oh, I think I ought to be able to find enough work to keep him out of trouble." She stood to leave. "Ma'am," she said in Sarah's direction, tucking her hair up into her hat.

"You comin', boy?" Devlin asked as Matthew jumped up to follow her.

Sarah looped a sack of food around the saddle horn of her son's mount. "You do everything Miss Brown tells you, is that clear?"

"Yes, ma'am." The boy turned and spurred his horse to catch up with Devlin.

"Givin' ya last-minute instructions, was she?" Devlin smirked.

"She told me I should do everything you tell me, Miss Brown."

"Smart woman, only don't call me Miss Brown, makes me feel like a school marm, *which* I ain't." Devlin raised an eyebrow at the boy.

"But Mom calls you Miss Brown," Matt said, appearing confused.

"Well…" She searched her brain for an answer. "Guess that's 'cause she's a lady."

"You're a lady, too, though." Matt seemed even more confused.

Devlin threw her head back and laughed loudly. Looking over at the boy's face red face, she laughed again. Slapping his arm in a friendly gesture, she gave him a Cheshire cat grin.

"Trust me, son, I ain't no lady!"

It was midday by the time Devlin and her new companion stopped for a break. Devlin had to admit the boy had the makings of a good cattleman. He worked hard and never complained. Devlin appreciated the boy's silence, so different from his mother in that respect.

"Your mom always cook like this?" Devlin asked as they leaned against the rough bark of an oak tree.

"Yup," Matthew said with his mouth full. "Good, huh?"

"Damn good." Looking up suddenly from her meal, she grinned at Matthew. "Don't you start using language like that, boy, or your mom will take after me with one of those Winchesters she's got over the mantel."

Matthew laughed at Devlin. He drank from his canteen and silently watched her. His body was already sore, but he wasn't about to admit it. He liked being with her almost as much as he enjoyed going out with his father. There was something about the tall woman that put Matt at ease. He knew she might work him until he dropped, but he felt safe and protected around her.

Devlin had her eyes closed slightly, but she felt the weight of the boy's stare. He was a hard worker, that was for sure. Still, he had an uphill battle, his father already gone at his age.

A crack echoed through the air, and Devlin bolted upright waiting for the last reverberation to fade. The boy looked in her direction questioningly, but Devlin had already jumped to her feet.

"Get on your horse now," she said.

She didn't have to say it twice as the two jumped into their saddles and quickly rode back toward the cabin. Alto galloped along at full speed and quickly outpaced the boy's black gelding. It was as if the horse felt the waves of concern that flowed from Devlin. Devlin knew the sound of a Winchester rifle when she heard one.

Devlin pulled Alto up hard in front of the large barn, throwing dirt and rock into the air. Devlin, along with her young companion, hadn't been too far away from the cabin, but it was long enough for Sarah to have already replaced the prized Winchester back over the mantel.

Devlin threw her right leg over the saddle horn and

effortlessly slid from the mare's saddle, while Sarah and Hannah looked somewhat surprised at the two. Devlin followed Sarah's eyes and finally saw the culprit lying on his side near the chicken coop. Devlin walked over and nudged a large fox with the toe of her boot. Bending down, she sat back on her heels and whistled through her teeth.

"Good God, woman, you got him right between the eyes," Devlin said in a mixture of surprise and appreciation.

Devlin lifted the fox up by the scruff of the neck as Hannah shyly scooted closer to get a better look. Sarah smiled a small knowing smile. Devlin had surprised her by galloping into the ranch, but Sarah didn't say a word. She felt safe around the woman who made most grown men nervous. Because of Devlin's praise, Sarah also felt something she couldn't quite understand. She felt flattered. She felt an unexplainable heat creep up into her cheeks and she turned away, but not before Devlin saw the blush on her face.

"Contrary to popular belief, Miss Brown, I'm not completely helpless," Sarah said as she stepped inside the cabin.

Devlin just stood there, still holding the unfortunate chicken thief by the neck. "Boy, you remember why I told you not to swear in front of your mother?

"Yep." Matthew grinned. "So she wouldn't take after ya with her Winchester."

Devlin took a long look at the cabin, then at the fox, a bullet hole placed perfectly between the creature's eyes. "Boy, don't *ever* tell that woman it was me who taught you to swear!" Dev looked up at Matthew with a lopsided grin and winked. Just before she walked off to skin the animal, she let another low whistle of appreciation slip through her lips.

It was already late in the day. Devlin and Matt took turns riding over to the calving herd. Devlin had skinned the fox and showed the boy how to cure the pelt when Sarah's voice came up behind them, a tinge of concern in her tone.

"Miss Brown, I think we have visitors," Sarah said, looking

out across the plain.

Devlin never looked up from the animal skin she worked over. "Yeah, they've been out there for a while now. Probably trying to figure out if it's safe to ride in." She looked up at Sarah with a hint of mischief in her eye. "No doubt they've heard about your fine marksmanship skills." She returned to her chore.

Sarah gave her a smirk. "Then you're not worried?"

"No, ma'am. They're Choctaw. They probably want to trade...maybe need some beef."

"We have plenty. If they're hungry, we could cut out a side of beef for them."

"No," Devlin said more harshly than she had intended. Standing up, she explained in a softer voice. "They wouldn't accept it anyway. It would be like charity to them. Choctaw always trade. If you give them something, they have to give you something of equal value in return. If you give a Choctaw something in value that he can't possibly return, it would be a great insult. They'd go hungry before they'd accept charity."

"That doesn't make much sense," Sarah said without thinking.

Devlin looked intently at her. "It does to them. What doesn't make sense to them is why the white man came into their world and killed off all the buffalo, a creature that was always wild, free, and plentiful, only to replace it with a smaller, dumber version that we have to take care of. It doesn't make sense to them that we put fences around land meant for everyone. What doesn't make sense to them is why we want to take a system that's worked just fine since the beginning of time and make it better."

Devlin finished and the two women stared at each other. Sarah saw that fire rage again in Devlin's eyes, and she realized how immature her statement had been. She brushed a lock of hair from her eye and looked contrite as she glanced up at Devlin.

"I'm sorry. That was a pretty arrogant thing to say. I spoke without thinking."

Before Sarah had finished, Devlin's gaze softened. Devlin looked into Sarah's angelic face and felt her own heart miss a beat. Her icy stare melted, and one corner of her mouth curled upward into a half-smile.

"Guess it's hard to keep track of your words when you say so many of them," Devlin teased, lifting her Stetson and running her hand through her hair, replacing it with a jaunty air.

Sarah opened her mouth for a sharp reply but immediately closed it. She looked over at Devlin and saw the smile on her face. It was the first time she'd seen Devlin display such a sparkling smile, and she felt her heart flutter. *She's absolutely beautiful when she smiles like that. Okay, where did that come from?* Sarah pushed the thought from her mind and slapped Devlin on the arm.

"Very funny. You won't be smiling when you have to make your own breakfast in the morning!" She laughed and walked toward the corral.

Good, God...did she just hit me? It took Dev a heartbeat for it to register, but she heard the sound of her own laughter as she followed the young woman.

"What are they waiting for?" Sarah asked, leaning against the fence rail.

"An invitation. They won't come in if they aren't welcome. The Choctaw are an amiable people. If I'm not around, that's one way you'll know it's them. They'll never ride up to the cabin unless they already know you. They never steal or demand. They'll always try to trade."

"How can I tell the friendly Indians from the hostile ones?"

Devlin furrowed her brow. "You'll know," she said soberly. "So do you want to meet your neighbors?"

"Yes, please."

While Sarah's head was turned, Devlin afforded herself the luxury of smiling at the excitement she heard in Sarah's voice.

Devlin felt a swell of appreciation develop. Sarah sounded as though she was naturally a kind-spirited woman.

Grabbing her hat by the brim, Devlin waved the party in the distance closer.

"*Halito*," Devlin said to the older man leading the party.

"*Halito, chim achukma, Redhawk*," the old man returned.

Sarah stared open-mouthed at Devlin, who carried on a conversation in another language with the eldest of the group of men. Sarah had suspected that the woman beside her knew just about everything and everyone in the Oklahoma Territory, but now Sarah was certain of it.

"*Illapa yamma*, Sarah Tolliver," Dev said, introducing the young woman. "Close your mouth and say hello."

"H-hello," Sarah stammered.

"*Halito*," Dev said the word slowly.

Sarah repeated the word, looking up at the old man and smiling sweetly.

"*Redhawk, atok ohoyo pisa aiukli*," the old man said to Devlin with a smile, prompting laughter from the other men.

Devlin's gaze darted back and forth from Sarah to the band of Indians, a hot flush rising up to her face.

"What did he say?" Sarah asked, noticing the tinge of color on Devlin's bronze cheeks.

"He's just trying to be funny." Devlin arched an eyebrow in the old man's direction.

Sarah heard a sound behind her. She turned to find Matthew and Hannah standing in the doorway of the cabin, their mouths as far open as Sarah's had been. She called them to her.

Devlin introduced Matthew but seemingly ignored Hannah, who clung to her mother's skirt.

A young Indian boy, not much older than Matthew, nudged his horse closer and looked down at Matt. The Indian boy stared at the knife strapped to Matthew's belt. He wore the knife on his hip, just as Devlin had showed him to do earlier in the day.

Devlin watched the exchange between the two young men.

"Come here, boy," she called, positioning Matthew in front of her. Devlin rested her hands on the boy's shoulders, lifting her head to speak to the boy on horseback.

"*Hachi banna amo bashpo?*" Devlin asked, motioning toward the boy's knife.

He was young but tried to hide his excitement. "*Akat.*" He nodded.

"He wants to trade you for your knife, boy," Devlin said to Matt.

"Trade for what?" Matt asked.

"That's your call. You've got to see if he's got something you want as bad as he wants your knife."

Devlin kept her voice, as well as her face, impassive while giving the boy instruction. That way, it would appear as if she was only translating languages. It was important to the Choctaw that a boy Matthew's age already be able to bargain effectively. It seemed important to Devlin that these men take him seriously.

"He's got a swell belt on," Matt finally said.

"You think you like it well enough to give away a knife for?"

"Well, I don't think I could ever make one like it."

Devlin liked the way the boy thought out the trade. A good trade wasn't always for something you needed right then, but something you couldn't get any other way. It would take many years for Matt to learn to weave a beaded belt such as the one this brave's mother or sister probably gave him. Likewise, the metal blade of Matt's knife was a coveted item among Indians because there wasn't any way they could walk into a white man's store and buy one, even if they did have the money.

"Pull out the knife and say the word *akat*. That means yes," Devlin said, watching as the boy did as instructed.

The brave smiled and slid from his horse, holding his empty hands out, palms facing upward.

"He wants to know what he has that you want," Devlin said.

Matt pointed to the intricately beaded leather belt the other boy wore around his waist.

The brave smiled broadly. *"Katihmi hinlatuk am itatoba sa na fehna askufachi."* He pointed to his belt. *"Isht hachim bashpo?"* He pointed to the knife.

"He wants to know why he should trade such a wonderful gift for your knife."

Matthew didn't know what to say, but he didn't want to look at Devlin for help. He had a feeling that might look like he didn't know what he was doing to these strangers.

"You need to show him that it's a good knife. Show him how sharp it is," Devlin said. "Hold your hand palm down and run the blade lightly across the top of your hand. He wants to see how it cuts."

As soon as the words were out of Devlin's mouth, Sarah attempted to take a step forward to stop the boy's actions. Devlin's hand shot out and grasped the woman's arm above her wrist, holding her in place. Sarah stared at Devlin, but Devlin didn't return the look. She gave Sarah's arm a gentle squeeze, not removing her hand, but letting her fingers rest lightly around Sarah's forearm. She tried to stay focused when all she wanted to do was close her eyes and give in to the temptation to caress the soft skin beneath her fingertips. Instead, she held the woman's arm against the outside of her thigh and tried to concentrate on the outside world.

Sarah was terrified at what Devlin had asked her son to do. She attempted to put a stop to it when Devlin's hand reached out and restrained her. Sarah's first reaction had been to pull away from the woman's grasp, but when Devlin tenderly squeezed her arm, Sarah's breath caught in her chest. She tried to ignore the tingling sensation she felt where Devlin held her. When Matt sliced a light cut across the top of his hand, Sarah reached up and wrapped her fingers into the strong ones of Devlin.

As the older men nodded their approval of Matthew's trade technique, Devlin focused on gathering air into her lungs. All involuntary movement in her body had halted the moment Sarah entwined her soft fingers into Devlin's calloused hand.

Once the two boys exchanged their goods, Devlin felt the small hand within her own relax, but she made no move to pull away. Devlin shook her head to get back to the reality of the situation.

"Now hold out your hand and shake hands by grabbing onto his forearm," Devlin instructed.

Once the boys shook hands Indian style, they considered the deal final. Everyone congratulated both boys on a good trade. Again, the older Indian appeared to watch the interaction between Sarah and Devlin with some interest. He took notice of Sarah's hand held firmly in the grasp of Devlin.

"*Redhawk, atok ohoyo pisa aiukli, aikuli tokba,*" the older Indian said to Devlin, again to smiles from the other braves.

Devlin stood her ground this time, neither turning red nor releasing the gentle grip she had on Sarah's hand. Straightening to her full height, she looked into the old man's eyes. "*Oktanichi aha aiashachi.*" She tapped her chest with a slender finger, her lips pulled back into a feral smile. "*Sarah yamma sa.*" Devlin finished by pointing to all the braves in the party saying, "*Aiena am na kashapa nana yamma sa.*"

Sarah watched the exchange and knew the conversation had something to do with her. She could see that Devlin had taken control of a situation, which involved Sarah, but she couldn't grasp any of the language. Suddenly, Sarah's eyes grew wide with understanding. She then saw the hungry stares some of the young men directed toward her. Watching Devlin's body language, Sarah listened to the tone of possessiveness in Devlin's voice. No language barrier existed when it came to emotions, and Sarah didn't need a translator to tell her that Devlin had effectively warned the men that Sarah was a woman already spoken for.

The braves laughed aloud. An older man slapped a tall, muscular young man, who had stared at Sarah during their entire visit, on the back.

"*Redhawk's ohoyo!*" He laughed again at the embarrassed youth, who winced when the older man bumped up against his left arm.

Sarah gasped loudly and Devlin's hand tensed involuntarily around Sarah's hand. They both saw that the sleeve of the brave's buckskin was colored in blood, which began to drip from the scarlet-soaked leather.

"You're hurt," Sarah said to the young man on the horse with concern.

Then, before Devlin could hold the woman back, she slipped away and moved to the injured brave. Sarah reached her hand out and tenderly examined the wounded arm. Sarah had the brave's hand in her own before Devlin could reach her.

The young man had a look that was nothing short of terror on his face, not daring to insult the forward woman by pulling away. The brave's eyes pleaded with Devlin, however, and Devlin gently pulled Sarah's hand away.

"But…" Sarah looked up at the Indian, then back to Devlin. "He needs help." Sarah stared at Devlin, who made no move to explain.

"Oh, I know. Let me guess. I can't touch him because I'm a woman!" Sarah exclaimed, a flash of her customary temper showing through as her eyes sparked.

Devlin wanted to laugh at the priceless expression of righteous indignation on Sarah's face. "Yes, but it's not for the reasons you're thinking," she explained. "You're an unmarried woman. In his eyes, it's beneath you to tend to his wounds."

Devlin recognized the confusion on Sarah's face. Looking down at her boots, Devlin swallowed hard when she realized once again that she still held the woman's smaller hand within her own. "Mrs. Tolliver…Sarah, these people hold women in very high esteem, especially unmarried women. This isn't about putting women down, it's about respect. They respect you." She didn't know any better way to explain and hoped she had gotten her message across.

Staring into Devlin's fixed gaze, Sarah felt embarrassed at having lost her temper so quickly, but that thought disappeared when she saw Devlin's eyes narrow. Sarah felt Devlin's pulse quicken under her fingertips. When Sarah looked down, she noted that she had absently begun to stroke the outside of Devlin's hand with her thumb.

All the air in Devlin's lungs disappeared. She stood completely unaware of the people around her, so lost to the pleasurable sensation of Sarah's fingers stroking her skin. Devlin attempted to open her mouth to speak, but speech left her when she saw Sarah looking at their hands. To Devlin, Sarah appeared aware that she had been caressing Devlin's wrist. Devlin knew that if she didn't stop it now, she'd quickly do something that would humiliate her, Sarah, or the both of them. With agonizing slowness, she unwillingly extricated her hands from the smaller ones that continued their feather-light touches.

The reality was that mere seconds had ticked by during the exchange, but to Devlin and Sarah, each trapped in her own emotions, time went on forever. One of the horses shook its head, the bridle jingling against his neck. The sound pulled the two women back into the present world, remembering the injured young man.

"I'm a widow. Doesn't it count if I was married once?" Sarah asked Devlin.

It took her a second to get her head back to their previous place in the conversation. "You're not married now. All they see is that you're without a mate."

Sarah smirked up at Devlin, arching an eyebrow as she did. It was frustration that led her to what she said next. "I would have thought you handled that when you told them I belonged to you."

Devlin froze. "I...uh...but I..." She was at a loss. Devlin couldn't figure out how Sarah had known. She didn't think Sarah would discover that she had told the Choctaw men Sarah belonged to her. What was worse, she had warned the men that she never shared what belonged to her. Sarah may have guessed at Devlin's meaning when talking to the men, but Devlin was certain Sarah didn't understand why.

"It's all right, and I really do understand. Otherwise, I'd have a brave knocking on my door every day, right?"

Devlin smiled in relief. "Yeah," Devlin whispered. She was barely able to admit to herself how satisfying it felt to lay claim to the beautiful young woman standing beside her.

"It does look like he's hurt rather badly." Sarah brought their attention back to the situation. "Isn't there any way we can help him?"

Devlin knew she wasn't going to win this one, but she was already getting used to Sarah's grit and determination wearing her down. She turned back to where the Indian sat astride his horse. "*Hacha ishkanapa a hachim shakba*?" Devlin asked the young man, indicating he should pull up his sleeve.

The brave spoke to Devlin as Sarah stood on her tiptoes to look over Devlin's shoulder. Dev felt Sarah's warm breath on her neck and a shiver ran the length of her body.

"He said a bear attacked their hunting party in the woods yesterday. Said the animal's claws did this. He's pretty proud of the fact he was the hunter who killed it."

"Bear claws can cause an infection. Besides, two of those cuts need sewing up," Sarah said.

"I'm good with herbs, but I'm not much with a needle and thread."

"I am. I've done it a lot over the years."

"Okay, let's see if we can get him to go for it."

Devlin talked to the brave until she was close to losing the last bit of patience she had. Cajoling and pleading didn't work. He steadfastly refused to have Sarah treat him. Devlin even rolled up her own shirtsleeve, exposing a long thin scar that ran from her elbow to her wrist.

"What did you say to him?" Sarah asked.

"I told him you sewed this one up for me and I lived."

"But I didn't."

Arching an eyebrow, Devlin rolled her eyes at the same time. "Work with me here, okay?"

"Oh," Sarah said with sudden realization.

Still the brave refused, and Devlin, never having been known for her patience, threw her hands up in the air.

"*Hachim fehnachi ahi abi hachi kanimichi!*" she spat at the young man.

"Do I want to know what that means?" Sarah asked.

"I told him that sooner or later his pride would kill him."

A thought occurred to Sarah. She had learned how to play the game with men because if there was one thing a man valued over all else, it was his pride. "Tell him I don't think he's much of a man," Sarah said to Devlin.

Devlin looked at Sarah as if she'd lost her mind. "See that bow slung across his back, Mrs. Tolliver? It ain't there for decoration. You want to be pullin' an arrow out of my chest?"

"That won't happen if I say it and you simply translate for me. Or are you more worried about how it will look to the men who think I belong to you?" Sarah folded her arms across her chest and stared back at Devlin.

"Okay, maybe I am. It…well, it'll look like I can't control you!" Devlin hissed through clenched teeth. Again, she knew she was fighting a losing battle. "Oh, all right! What was it again?" She turned to the brave and translated as Sarah spoke.

"I don't think you're much of a man. I had heard that Choctaw men were brave and proud. I see I must have misunderstood, seeing as how you're too big a coward to let a woman touch you."

Devlin nearly choked on the words as she repeated them, but Sarah's words affected the young man. He looked at his comrades, who looked as if they wondered if it wasn't respect he felt for the unmarried woman or if he was just frightened of her.

Sarah continued on with her carefully planned humiliation until the other men in the party teased and laughed at the young man. Suddenly, the brave jumped down from his horse and pulled his buckskin shirt over his head. Standing in front of Sarah, he pointed to his arm.

"*Aiiskiachi*!" he demanded.

Devlin gave a warning look to the young man.

The brave took a step backward and lowered his head toward Sarah. "*Asilhha*," he said.

Devlin smiled at Sarah "He says to fix it…please."

By the time Sarah had finished with wrapping a bandage around the young man's arm, Devlin walked her way with an armload of goods she had obtained from the others by way of trade.

"Do you have any sugar and flour to spare?" Devlin asked.

"Of course. How much do you want?"

"Just a small sack of each. How about some smoked or salted beef?"

By the time Sarah gathered all the requested items, Devlin had returned to her bartering session with the group.

The setting sun glowed orange against the backs of the Indian party as they rode away. It was a good day of trading for Kontonalah and his party, and the old man enjoyed himself. He rarely went on trading parties anymore, but he had been as curious about the small woman they had watched from afar as the rest of the members of the Thunderbird clan. When reports of her standing alone in the darkness, speaking aloud to the spirits of the night sky had reached them, it impressed the clan elders. Women rarely talked to the spirits. White women never did. Keeho, the clan healer, said she harbored strong medicine.

Late one night, after they had offered prayers and the sacred tobacco smoke had gone up to the great spirit, Keeho told of seeing the white woman marking messages down onto parchment. She then tied them to dried clumps of sagebrush, using the wind to send them on to the spirits. Keeho said that was why she had not suffered the ravages of winter as the white men around her had.

Kontonalah chuckled to himself. He believed in the spirits, of course, but he wasn't sure it was all the spirits' doing that had saved the woman's stock. He had left the warmth of his own fire on occasion to watch her, dressed in the clothes of a brave, doing a brave's work. He watched her trudge through snow that nearly swallowed her up, breathe on frozen fingers to keep them working, and wrestle with the small buffalo-like beasts to keep them alive. He felt that her hard work had been most of the reason she had fared so well. He wouldn't insult Keeho or the spirits by saying it aloud, however.

It was always a treat to see Redhawk. Now what was the name the white man gave her? Ah, yes, Devlin. Redhawk suited her much better. She was more at peace than Kontonalah had ever seen her, and he smiled to himself, thinking much of it had to do with the woman called Sarah. What had Keeho's vision named her? *Sakli*, Little Salmon. It was hard remembering things these days. It seemed as though he could remember events from long ago as if they had just happened but had a harder time with events that happened moments before. Now where was he in his ramblings?

Little Salmon. It was unprecedented to name someone who wasn't yet a member of the Thunderbird clan, but Keeho had the gift of vision and no one could argue with that. The healer said he saw the young woman's totem as a fish, the *sakli* that was always trying to swim upstream. Again, he chuckled. The vision fit with the reality of the young woman he had just met. He saw the fire in her eyes and witnessed more than Redhawk thought, watching the two women interact. Yes, this one would be good for Redhawk.

Kontonalah allowed his smile to reach his face this time. It was about time that his granddaughter had found a heart able to ease her pain. The old man smiled because he knew that *hasimbish humma* and *sakli*, the Redhawk and the Salmon, always made a good match.

Chapter Four

Devlin watched the trading party until dusk and the misty horizon swallowed them up. She scooped up the additional items she had traded the dry goods and beef for, heading toward the cabin. Devlin stopped at the open door, unable to walk through without an invitation. Seeing Sarah's smile, however, Devlin entered with her arms loaded with goods.

Sarah leaned over the fireplace, stirring a thick stew in a large cast iron pot. "Looks like you had a good day at the market," she said, watching Devlin lay her bundle on the table.

"Two horse blankets, two horse-hair halters, and a lead rope. Boy, take this stuff and put it in the barn," Devlin ordered. "Got something I want to show you when you get back."

It surprised Sarah when her son picked up the goods and carried out Devlin's request without question.

Sarah replaced the heavy lid on the cast iron pot after dropping in some dumplings to steam on top of the stew, her hand lightly brushing Hannah's cheek as she stood. The girl sat on a stool with her head down, staring into the fire. Her legs swung back and forth, her feet kicking against the stone hearth.

"Someone feels a little neglected today," Sarah said softly.

"Wondered if that would happen." Devlin looked up with an apologetic smile. "Actually, I'm kind of surprised you didn't fight me on it at the time."

"I guess so many other things were happening that I lost

track," Sarah said. "So is there a reason?"

"I told you the Choctaw hold unmarried women in high esteem. That goes tenfold for girls under the age of womanhood. Girls can't talk to any men of the tribe unless they're related to them. Consequently, men don't speak to girls until they reach an age of maturity. It keeps…" A small look of pain made itself visible on Devlin's face. "It keeps unfortunate things from happening to young girls."

"We could learn a few things from them," Sarah said, not taking her eyes off her daughter. "I like these friends of yours, Miss Brown."

Devlin smiled. It was a slow, easy smile, the kind she had become accustomed to displaying around this woman and her family.

"And they like you, Mrs. Tolliver. Now they're your friends, too. Excuse me for just a minute, please." Devlin lowered herself to sit cross-legged on the floor beside Hannah.

"Hey, girl." She tilted her head to make eye contact with her. "Our friends gave me a present to give to you. Wanna see it?"

"For me?" Hannah asked, brightening.

"Uh-huh." Devlin reached into her vest pocket and pulled a small thin necklace made of tiny blue beads. Devlin held the necklace up before the girl's face and watched her green eyes go wide.

"Ooh…pretty."

Devlin slipped the beads over the girl's head and leaned back to take in her delight. Without warning, Hannah leapt from the stool and into Devlin's lap. Wrapping her arms around Devlin's neck, Hannah kissed her cheek. She then settled herself comfortably in Devlin's lap.

Sarah was about to rescue the shocked Devlin when Hannah turned in Devlin's lap and rested her back against Devlin's chest. Devlin lifted the necklace so the girl could make a closer inspection of her gift, launching into a story about how a tiny girl about Hannah's age made the water in the lake turn blue with her pretty blue beads.

Once Devlin had finished her story, Sarah smiled and confronted Devlin. "I thought you said the Choctaw never gave gifts."

"There are two exceptions to that rule." She gently rocked Hannah in her lap. "First exception, little girls." Devlin kissed the top of Hannah's head, causing the girl to snuggle deeper into Devlin's embrace. "Since the men can't pay much attention to them, they make them gifts. That way, little girls grow up to feel special and well loved. The second exception is when the gift is left by a spirit."

"A spirit?"

"Well, actually, someone leaves the gift, but you have to be good enough not to let anyone see you. It's an insult not to accept a gift from the spirits." Devlin paused, sliding Hannah gently off her lap. "Speaking of gifts, I thought you deserved something for the way you handled yourself today. Not a lot of women would have helped that young man the way you did." Devlin pulled a small square of cloth from her shirt pocket. Separating the fabric, she lifted up a necklace, holding it out to Sarah.

"I don't deserve a gift just for being kind," Sarah said, a blush creeping up her neck. "Besides, shouldn't I be insulted by you trying to give me a gift?" She finished by smiling at Devlin.

"You're not Choctaw. It doesn't apply." Devlin returned a smile of her own. She took Sarah's hand, placing the decorative necklace in her palm.

Sarah held the necklace up to the light to examine it. The string consisted of tiny shells strung with pale beads in between, a small greenish-blue stone hung from its center.

"It's beautiful," Sarah said breathlessly. She turned her back to Devlin. "Would you tie it for me?"

Devlin reached over the smaller woman and took the necklace in her own hands, each arm around Sarah's shoulder. Sarah reached up and swept her hair across one shoulder.

Devlin's uncharacteristically trembling fingers tied the ends of the necklace closed.

Sarah turned to the mirror, Devlin's reflection behind her. She felt the smooth texture of the stone beneath her fingers. "I don't think I've ever owned anything quite as beautiful. What kind of stone is this?" She glanced up at Devlin's image in the mirror.

"The Indians call it *okchako-talia*. It means blue stone. The Choctaw believe that if you receive *okchako-talia* as a gift, your dreams will be filled with visions of your heart's desire."

Suddenly, Peter's words came back to her. *"Sarah, next time, don't settle for less than your heart's desire."*

Devlin's gaze locked with Sarah's, and they stood in silence, staring at the other's reflection. The sound of the coffeepot bubbling over wrenched Sarah from her thoughts. She pulled the coffee off the stove's cooking plate just as Matthew entered the cabin. By that time, Devlin knelt beside Hannah once more, teasing and tickling the girl's stomach, which caused peals of laughter from the youngster. Without pausing or lifting her head, Devlin spoke to the boy.

"Did you make sure your mother has enough firewood split?"

"Yes, ma'am."

"Good man." Devlin stood and lifted Hannah over one shoulder before settling the still giggling girl to the floor.

Sarah watched as her son's chest puffed out ever so slightly. It was the first time that she had heard Devlin call him anything but boy.

Devlin lifted up her vest and pulled out a leather pouch tucked into her belt. She tossed it toward Matthew. "This ought to keep ya from missing the other one too bad."

Matt opened the pouch and a shrill whistle passed through his front teeth. "What's it made from?"

"Deer antler. See how they sharpen this half into a blade, then they leave the other part untouched so it acts like a curved handle? It won't last as long as a metal blade, but it's every bit as sharp as your other knife, so don't go cuttin' your fingers off. Let me know if you get a chip in it and I'll show you how to carve it out."

"Dinner is ready. Go wash up," Sarah said.

Watching the three traipse outside, Devlin stooping down to scoop Hannah into her arms, Sarah felt a twinge of unexplainable happiness. She didn't know why she experienced such a comforting feeling around Devlin, nor could she explain the heat that enveloped her body when Devlin's fingers had brushed against her neck when tying the piece of jewelry. Again, Sarah fingered the smooth stone around her neck. For the time being, she decided not to question any of it. She couldn't explain it, but she didn't want to spoil it

Devlin sat outside in the darkness, her chair tilted back on two legs against the cabin, when Sarah walked out.

"I think we deserve this, don't you?" Sarah asked as she held out two cups to Devlin, pouring from a bottle of Kentucky bourbon.

"Yes, ma'am." Dev sat up immediately.

Sarah sat on a chair beside Devlin and took a sip of the smooth whiskey. Leaning her back against the cabin, she closed her eyes and let the warm night breeze wash over her.

Devlin enjoyed the sight immensely. She liked the moments when she could gaze at Sarah without having to sneak looks out of the corner of her eye. She decided to break their silence.

"It meant a lot to those people today, the kindness you showed them. They'll never forget it." Devlin wondered if she should tell Sarah any of what Kontonalah had told her the Thunderbird clan believed regarding Sarah.

"I hope they won't forget me. I'll certainly never forget them. Do you know where they live? Do you think I could ever meet any of the women?" Sarah asked with a touch of excitement.

"Yes, I do, and perhaps," Devlin said with a mysterious half-smile.

"Miss Brown…"

Devlin closed her eyes. She knew what was coming. She had only hoped it wouldn't be so soon. What could she do other than to tell the truth? Devlin felt as though she owed no less to Sarah. *Great spirit, I know I don't talk to you much, but please, have a heart. I've been trying, haven't I?*

"How did you learn to speak the Choctaw language?"

Still Devlin waited, feeling as though the inevitable question would come. "I lived with them a very long time ago." She looked across at Sarah and knew she wasn't going to get away with any one-line answers.

Sarah turned in her seat, tucking her legs under her and draping an arm across the back of her chair in preparation for the rest of the story. She stared back into Devlin's face with an unwavering gaze, silently asking Devlin to continue.

Devlin cleared her throat, her eyes looking into the darkness. "It's been…maybe twenty years ago now. I was hurt pretty bad. Got caught doing the kind of thing that usually gets a reckless, wild kid killed. *Oh, for God sakes, just tell her you were an outlaw!* I was only thirteen, but I'd already joined up with a bad bunch. I was shot up and had more broken bones than I could count, thought I was dead for sure. I don't much remember how I even got there, but when I came to, someone was taking care of me. They never asked for a thing, just saw a kid who needed help.

"I stayed with them for a long time after I was healed. Kind of grew up there. Part of me wanted to be like them, like the kind of people they were. Only problem was back then, there was a part of me that couldn't let go of all that hate. So after about ten years, I left."

"Ten years? No wonder you speak the language so well. Do you think you could teach me, so I can speak for myself?"

"If you'd like." *Come on, is that all? Don't you want to ask the question everyone asks? Don't you want to know how many people I've killed…the horrible and cruel things I've done? Don't you want to ask me if it's all true?*

"I heard them use the name Redhawk. Is that what they call you?"

"Yes." Devlin couldn't stand the waiting. "Mrs. Tolliver, haven't you ever heard any of the stories about me?" Devlin held her breath.

"Good, God..." Sarah laughed. "I think I've heard *all* the stories about you!"

Devlin looked at her with astonishment. "Aren't you afraid? Afraid to have me near your children, sleeping right outside your house?"

Sarah rested her head in the palm of her hand. "I don't know the woman you seem to think I should be so frightened of." Sarah paused to take a sip of her drink. "Do you know what kind of a woman I was, Miss Brown?"

Devlin shook her head.

"I was a spoiled brat that someone should have taken in hand before I was allowed to hurt so many people. My mother died when I was a year old and I became a Southern belle who ended up getting everything I asked for because my father couldn't say no to me. I used emotional blackmail to get my father to teach me how to shoot, ride, and tend cattle. It effectively ended any chance I ever had at finding a husband. I was so selfish, I denied my father a chance at love and happiness because I didn't want to have to compete with any woman for his affections. I thought it bad enough that I had a sister who shared his love.

"He died in the war, never knowing how much I truly admired, respected, and loved him. I was intelligent, and I knew it. I had a sharp tongue and a sharper temper, and I used both every chance I got. I married a man who knew I never loved him. I used him to fulfill my own dream of coming out west." Sarah stopped as tears filled her eyes.

"You see, I don't think you would have liked the woman I was back then, and I expect I wouldn't have liked the woman you were very much. So when we hear they're giving out new pasts, I'll let you know and we can both get in line." She finished with a sad smile, taking another large gulp of the drink in her hand.

Devlin couldn't bear to look at the unhappy woman; her tears broke Devlin's heart. When Devlin looked across at Sarah, she spied a tear rolling down her cheek and without thinking reached out to brush it away. Sarah took Devlin's hand and held it in her lap, as both women struggled to find the necessary air to continue.

"I don't know that other woman you used to be, but I like the woman you are now," Devlin whispered.

"And I like the woman you are. I'd like to think of you as more than just someone who works here. I'd like to think of you as...well, as my friend," Sarah said, giving Devlin's hand a squeeze.

Devlin offered a lopsided grin. "I'd like that, too." *Oh, Sarah, I want you as my friend, but I want so much more than that. I'll never betray your trust, though. If friendship is all you're offering, I'll treasure it for the rest of my life.*

"Look, a shooting star. Quick, make a wish," she said with childish enthusiasm and a sparkle in her eye.

Dev closed her eyes. *It's already come true, my friend. It's already come true.*

Chapter Five

Devlin worked hard on the Double Deuce, taking her job seriously. She and Sarah eventually formed an easygoing working relationship. Sarah tried to adhere to rule number one, allowing Devlin do her job without question, and Devlin tried not to bristle when Sarah forgot about rule number one.

Devlin rode particularly far one day to nearly the edge of Double Deuce land. There had been a cut in the herd they had pastured on the far ridge. Not everyone would have noticed, but to Devlin's trained eye, they were short by no less than twenty head of cattle. She followed the signs until finding what she expected.

Hellfire! Devlin cursed to herself, looking down into the valley below. A small herd of cows had been corralled, unattended. She removed her outer jacket and tucked it under the saddle behind her. Pulling both pistols from her holster, she proceeded to check each, assuring herself of a full load.

Riding into the herd, she pushed one of the large cows in the rump, causing the animal to turn its branded hip toward Devlin. The brand felt too raised, an indication the animal had been double branded. It was also the brand of a double letter Z. The brand Sarah used, the number two, closely overlapped by another number two, had obviously been cleverly covered up by this newer brand. Dev started to move the cows out when a voice came from behind her.

"Where the hell ya think yer goin' with that herd?"

Devlin turned her horse to find herself about fifteen feet

away from the grizzled cowboy that had lost five dollars to Hank because he bet against Devlin's return from the snowstorm. Just to his right was the young man she had kicked out of her bunk the night of the snowstorm, sitting astride his mare looking around nervously.

"These cows belong to the Double Deuce, and that's where they're going." She looked up at the two men, watching their eyes and body language.

"It'd be best if you just minded yer own business. We don't want trouble with you, Brown," the younger man said, his voice cracking slightly.

"I ride for the Double Deuce. That makes rustlin' their cows my business. Boy, you actually thought about what you're doing here?"

"I can take care of myself."

"Look, I don't want to kill you and you'd like bein' dead even less. Why don't we just chalk this one up to a mistake and we'll go our separate ways?"

Devlin had her brim pulled low. She could see the reactions in the eyes of the men across from her, but the hat's shadow covered her blue eyes. For a few seconds, they stared at one another that way, but Dev knew they wouldn't be able to let it go. Men! They always thought if there was more of them, they'd be able to take her. It only meant one thing to Devlin... more dead bodies.

It was a small twitch, but Devlin saw it. The older man looked at something just over Dev's left shoulder. Devlin heard it then, soft like a whisper. It was a horse hoof in the dirt. Devlin didn't have the luxury of waiting for the men in front of her to make the first move. Carefully and without drawing attention, Devlin slipped her left foot out of the stirrup and pushed the right stirrup forward until only the ball of her foot rested there. Even over the sound of the cattle, she heard the faint click of metal behind her.

With one swift movement, Devlin launched her body over the side of her horse. In mid-air, she pulled both guns from their holster and let loose a blaze of gunfire on the two men in front of her. Tucking into a tight ball as soon as she hit the ground, she rolled twice, pulling herself up to crouch behind a cow. She looked up and saw the two men who had confronted her dead on the ground. The third man's saddle was empty, but there was no body to account for his whereabouts.

"Hellfire," she cursed again, reloading her gun. It was beginning to get dark, and she could barely see a thing, let alone a man coming at her. An explosion rang out and she could feel the air blow by her, a bullet narrowly missing her head. Devlin saw the fire of an explosion in the darkness and tried to ease toward it the long way. Cows and horses moved against her in the darkness. She saw the shadow too late.

A loud exchange rang in her ears as the man fired his gun, and Devlin felt a white-hot bolt of pain sear through her abdomen. She was unable to keep her knees locked against the pain, and they crumpled underneath her.

Devlin's brain told her to get up, but her body couldn't cooperate. She lay face down in the dirt, trying to still her rapidly pounding heartbeat. She heard the man come up behind her, bending down to pull her fallen body over. She brought her knee up hard into the man's face as he rolled her over, screaming at the pain in her gut the action caused. He fell to the ground, hands covering his broken nose and blood spilling from between his fingers. Dragging her body up, Devlin twisted around and pulled the trigger into the man's stomach.

She struggled to her feet, whistling for Alto. The horse walked up next to the woman and stopped. Dev put her hand to her side, pulling it away to see it covered in blood.

"Shit!" She tried to take a step forward and dropped to one knee.

Heaving herself up by pulling on Alto's stirrup, she was able to stand again. The man behind her came to just as she made a supreme effort to mount the huge mare.

"I thought I killed you," he groaned.

"That was your second mistake." She winced in pain as she

fell into the saddle.

"Mind tellin' me what the first mistake was?"

"Fucking with me in the first place." She moaned, her head bent over the pale mare's neck.

Her sarcasm was lost on the fallen man. He was already dead.

Sarah had begun to worry more and more. By now, she was downright afraid, but she tried not to show it in front of Hannah and Matthew. Devlin hadn't come back to the ranch the night before. That happened when wranglers were out on the range, but when it started to turn dark again that evening, her concern turned to fear. Sarah stood in the middle of the cabin dressed in a shirt and pants, pulling on a heavy jacket. Matthew saddled Telemachus, the black racing stallion Sarah had raised herself.

"Mom!" Matthew yelled from the corral.

Sarah ran to where her son stood and followed his gaze out into the growing darkness. It looked like a horse, but she couldn't tell from that distance. The boy held the reins as his mother swiftly pulled herself into the saddle.

Sarah pulled the black horse up abruptly in front of the large mare. Devlin barely hung on to Alto's saddle horn, and when the horse jerked to a stop, Devlin slipped from the mare's back. Jumping from her own mount, Sarah half caught, half felt Devlin fall on her.

Devlin's face was pale, dark circles colored the skin under her eyes, and she moaned in pain when her side pressed against Sarah's body. Sarah looked down at Devlin's shirt soaked in blood.

"Matt!" Sarah screamed. "Bring the wagon. Now!"

"Oh, God, Devlin…what happened to you?" Sarah cradled Devlin in her arms, impatiently waiting for the sound of the buckboard's wheels.

Devlin regained consciousness as Sarah and Matthew dragged her limp body into the cabin. Sarah tossed a blanket over the long kitchen table, and they eased her back until the long length of her body lay atop the table.

Unceremoniously, Sarah began ripping Devlin's shirt open, pulling up the cotton undergarment. She soaked a cloth in a bucket of water Matt had brought in, wiping away the worst of the bleeding so she could get a decent look at the wound. Devlin labored with each breath. She clenched her teeth together and grunted when Sarah pressed down on her side.

"Matthew..." Sarah turned and pulled open the top drawer from a large bureau. She lifted off the lid to a weathered oak box and pulled out a half-dozen sharp bladed instruments. "Take the small cooking pot outside and scrub it with lye soap, put clean water in it, and start it to boiling. Put these instruments in the water and let them boil for five minutes." Sarah moved to the mantel and pulled down her father's pocket watch.

"Use grandfather's watch and you'll be able to time five minutes. After that much time, take them out and bring them to me. Be careful, don't touch them with your hands once they're clean, and don't burn yourself. Then put fresh water on to boil, take this cloth, and tear it into strips about this wide." She motioned with her hands. "Boil them for a few minutes. Then come in and put the strips to dry on the rack by the fireplace. Can you do all that?"

"Yes, ma'am. Is she going to be all right?"

"If I have anything to say about it, she will," Sarah said with confidence, placing a gentle hand on his cheek.

Hannah peeked around the stairs that led to the loft where she and Matthew slept. Sarah went back into her bedroom to get one last, necessary item.

Devlin spied Hannah, turning her head toward the child's gasp of surprise.

"Are you hurt, Dev?" Hannah asked.

"Yeah," she whispered. "But I'll be all right, princess."

When Sarah returned, Hannah held Devlin's hand. Devlin whispered small assurances that she would be around in the morning. Sarah scooped the child up to carry her upstairs.

"But I want to kiss Devlin good night," the youngster

wailed.

Devlin looked up at the girl with a lopsided grin and crooked her finger to Sarah, motioning her closer. Hannah leaned down from her mother's arms and placed a kiss on Devlin's dirty cheek. Sarah deposited the youngster at the foot of the stairs.

"Hannah, I want you to be a big girl and go upstairs and get into bed. I don't want you coming down here again tonight, no matter what you hear. Is that understood?"

The girl nodded.

"And, Hannah…you've never disobeyed me and you won't now, either, will you?"

"No, Mama," the girl said seriously, walking up the stairs.

Devlin breathed hard against the pain, her eyes closed. Sarah brushed Devlin's damp bangs off her forehead. The wounded woman opened her eyes and looked into the face of an angel, green eyes staring intently into her own.

"Guess I got shot." She smirked.

"I guess you did," Sarah said with concern. "What happened?"

"Rustlers. You ought to see the other guys, though." Devlin smiled as much as she could, considering the circumstances.

"What happened to them?" Sarah asked, afraid of the answer.

"Dead." Devlin closed her eyes once more. "Sarah, you need to be careful. The rustlers were hired-hands from your uncle's ranch. Keep your eyes open and those Winchesters loaded. Send the boy to Mr. Winston's place in the morning, tell 'em what happened. If anything happens to me—"

"Nothing like that is going to happen!" Sarah steeled herself to gather focus for what she had to do. "That bullet's still in your side. What's worse, you've already started to develop an infection. Your skin feels like it's on fire right here." She placed her cool hand on the heated skin just above Devlin's hip. "That means you've got an abscess starting under the skin. We need to get that bullet out of you. My father taught me a lot. He was very good at what he did for a living."

Devlin's eyes opened quickly. "Just what did your father do for a living?"

Matthew brought in the boiled instruments wrapped in a towel, and Sarah scrubbed her hands with soap before taking them. She placed the instruments on the table next to the prone woman.

"He was a doctor."

Devlin took one look at the instruments, their blades gleaming brightly in the cabin's light, then looked back up at Sarah, then down to the instruments again.

"No, no, no, no!" Devlin tried to lift herself off the table, but in her weakened condition, Sarah easily held her down. "Look," Devlin said in a panic. "I've ridden worse things than this out before. I can do it again."

"Devlin, you will die of infection, period." Sarah took hold of Devlin's chin, willing the blue eyes to her own. "*Hachim fehnachi ahi abi hachi kanimichi!*" she said angrily, losing her temper.

Devlin's eyes narrowed as Sarah spoke the words she had used on the injured brave—*your pride will kill you one day.*

Sarah leaned over the injured woman and stroked her cheek and forehead, tears filling her eyes. "I don't want to lose you, Dev. I need you to trust me," Sarah whispered.

Devlin slowly closed her eyes and nodded to the young woman who had come to mean so much in her life.

Sarah pulled the cork on the bottle she'd retrieved from her bedroom, and after helping Devlin to lean up on one elbow, she handed it to her.

"Drink," Sarah ordered.

"What is it? Hellfire! It smells like kerosene."

"It tastes like it, too. Just drink," Sarah commanded as she pulled off her jacket and rolled up the sleeves to her shirt.

"Good God, woman! What is this stuff?" Devlin bellowed, feeling her first swallow burn all the way down her throat.

"Where I come from, it's called 'shine. Folks outside of Kentucky call it moonshine. It'll get you drunk in a hurry or clean rust off your tools. Three swallows and it'll knock you on your butt, so keep drinking." Sarah began to remove Devlin's garments. *It's a good thing I'm so damn scared right now because I don't even want to know why the sight of Devlin, naked from the waist up, is affecting me this way.*

Devlin had no inhibitions about her body and continued to drink the powerful liquor, even as Sarah removed her clothes. Matthew came in and placed the cleaned bandages by the fireplace to dry, lowering his head at the sight. Sarah walked over to her son and cleaned her hands with soap and water.

"I'm going to need your help, but I'll also need you to act like an adult and a gentleman. Do you understand?" The sight of the strong, beautiful woman had produced a powerful reaction in Sarah, so she could only guess at what it must be doing to her son. "I'll need you to try and hold her down when I take the bullet out. Think you can handle this?"

"Yes, ma'am." Matt swallowed as mother and son turned back to Devlin, half a bottle of the potent liquor inside the prone woman. Matt positioned himself on Devlin's right side. True to his word, he stared straight ahead.

Devlin felt very little by then, the hard liquor having gone straight to her head. She turned to look at Sarah, staring over the table at Sarah's figure, the curves of her lower body hugged tightly by pants.

"You look different," Devlin slurred, leering at Sarah and still holding on to the bottle of moonshine.

"Give me that." Sarah rolled her eyes at the now drunken woman.

The first incision went well, Devlin barely flinching at the pain. Sarah probed the area with her fingers, and Devlin nearly leapt from the table. She panted hard and Matthew rubbed an eye that, moments before, had come into contact with Devlin's fist. Sarah picked up a long set of tweezers and a thin needle-like probe. Her son saw what was coming and turned his head, nearly laying his whole body across Devlin's right side.

"This is going to hurt like hell, Dev."

"Do it." Devlin groaned, steeling herself against the pain.

Sarah felt the bullet about two inches deep. She tried to work quickly, but to the injured woman and the boy trying to hold down the six-foot woman, the seconds became infinity. Sarah's hands were sure, even with the jerking and thrashing, and she pulled the metal free from Devlin's body just before Devlin was convinced her jaw would snap from the tension of grinding her teeth so hard.

Devlin's chest heaved and she took in great gulps of air, desperately trying to fight down feelings of nausea. Her head became dizzy, and she felt a stinging sensation as Sarah cleaned the wound of any remaining infection. By the time Sarah sewed the wound closed, Devlin's world not only spun franticly, but she barely felt anything at all.

Sarah worked to wrap clean bandages around the wound. Along with her son, they managed to get Devlin onto Sarah's bed.

"Matt, heat up a couple of buckets of water for me, then head off to bed, all right?" Sarah said wearily. "You were a big help tonight. I couldn't have done that without you, son."

Matthew grinned tiredly at his mother and quickly went about supplying the hot water. After he left the requested water, Sarah sat alone with an unconscious Devlin. She removed the woman's clothes, using soap and water to cleanse the mud and blood from Devlin's body. She washed the woman's hair as best she could and changed the linen on the bed. Pulling the soft comforter up to Devlin's shoulders, Sarah tenderly ran her fingers through the still damp hair before turning away.

Sarah was bone tired, more so from fear and tension rather than the actual need for rest. She had just removed her shirt, clad only in her cotton camisole, when she heard a moan from the bed. Devlin moved and her eyes fluttered open but seemed unable to focus. Sarah came and sat on the edge of the bed.

"Devlin? Dev?" Sarah asked.

Devlin found her voice, taking in the exciting vision before her. "You look a lot different!" She leered at Sarah.

"You are drunk." Sarah laughed quietly.

"Oh, no," Devlin slurred her words. "If I was drunk, could I do this?"

Before Sarah had a chance to react, Devlin's hand shot up to the small of her back, pressing Sarah down against Devlin's chest. Devlin's mouth took possession of Sarah's before she had a chance to protest.

At first, Sarah was shocked and surprised. She felt Devlin's lips on her own, strong hands moving up to caress her face, then Devlin's tongue brushed lightly against lips that began to move involuntarily in response to Devlin's passion.

Devlin's arms once again encircled Sarah. Sarah knew she had to stop what was happening, but when the warmth of Devlin's tongue entered her mouth, she lost herself completely to the physical sensations. She not only allowed the kiss to happen, but somehow became a willing participant.

Devlin's mouth found its way to her earlobe, sucking on the tender flesh. "Oh, God, woman, I want you." Devlin groaned.

It had been so long since Sarah had experienced physical intimacy with anyone that her body betrayed her with a torrent of physical needs and desires, all of them suddenly met by the woman who now held Sarah in her arms.

Devlin's hand pressed firmly against Sarah's breast, her thumb stroking the nipple into a hardened point. Devlin took the young woman in another dizzying kiss, removing her hand from Sarah's chest. Devlin pulled the blanket down, just to the top of the dark curls between her legs. Grasping Sarah's small hand in her own, Devlin placed the young woman's hand over her own breast. She ran it along her torso until Sarah's fingers brushed the light down of hair below Devlin's abdomen, then Devlin pulled Sarah's hand back to her breast. She kneaded the hand under her own, pressing Sarah's fingers against a nipple already hardened and erect with desire.

Devlin's movements suddenly stopped as quickly as they began, her arm hitting the bed with a thump. The inebriated woman passed out, leaving Sarah's panting form somewhat relieved yet highly frustrated.

Sarah slipped from the bed to the floor, holding her head in her hands. "Good, God!" she moaned.

The next morning, Devlin couldn't remember when her head had ever felt so bad. It pounded like she'd been on a three-day drunk. She couldn't suppress the groan that escaped from her throat when she opened her eyes. Sunlight bathed the room in a white light.

Sarah jumped to her feet as soon as she heard Devlin's voice. She hastily pulled the shirt on that she had worn the previous evening. Every muscle in her back screamed after spending the night in the wooden rocking chair she had pulled into the bedroom.

Kneeling beside Devlin, Sarah's cool hand brushed away the dark locks from Devlin's face. Sarah still felt the fever within Devlin. Devlin's eyes opened, her soft gaze fixing on the smiling face of the woman above her.

"Hi." Sarah smiled.

"Why is it so damn bright in here?"

Sarah laughed and stood, moving to the window and pulling the heavy curtains across the opening. Devlin's body relaxed slightly, but the darkness hadn't done a thing for the pain in her head.

"Wasn't I shot in the gut?" Devlin whispered hoarsely.

"Pretty much."

"Then why does my head feel like it just got stomped by a bull?"

"Oh." Sarah looked down at Devlin guiltily. "I guess that was the moonshine."

"The moon...what?"

"Let me get you something for that head first." Sarah walked out of the bedroom and returned shortly with a cup, a pitcher of water, and a small bottle of colorless liquid. Quickly explaining about the liquor she had used as an anesthesia, Sarah poured Devlin a cup of water, placing a few drops of the clear liquid into the cup.

"This tastes bitter, but it's just a painkiller. It will make you sleepy, though."

"No. I need to get up," Devlin said, using all her strength just to move into a sitting position. The pain in her side felt like someone had just jabbed a hot poker into her middle. The groan of agony she let out then made her reach for her head to stop the throbbing there. Finally, she knew she'd been beat when Sarah was able to put both hands on her shoulders and effectively hold her down.

"Sarah!"

"Devlin!"

The two women stared daggers at each other, wondering who would break first. Devlin tried to intimidate Sarah with one of her infamous icy stares, but she quickly learned that the technique didn't seem to work if the person wasn't afraid of you in the first place.

"Oh, give it to me." Devlin held her hand out for the cup, then downed it all in two long swallows.

"Why is it that medicine that's supposed to be good for you always tastes so bad?" She groaned, making a face at the bitter-tasting liquid.

Sarah pushed Devlin farther under the covers, pulling them around her shoulders. "Well, the next time, I'll put some honey in it just like I do for Hannah. Would that make you feel better?" she asked with a saccharine sweetness.

"Yes," Devlin said with as close to a pout as six feet of former outlaw could get. "You're enjoying this, being in control, aren't you?"

"Relishing every moment of it," Sarah said with a wide grin.

Devlin realized at that moment that she was naked under the blanket. "Where are my clothes?"

"Oh. I had to take them off to...well, I was going to wash..."

Sarah looked down into Devlin's eyes, which looked up

with amusement at the stammering woman. Sarah became perturbed at herself for her reaction. She didn't like losing her composure, especially when she had been in full control seconds before.

Stopping to give Devlin a superior look, Sarah turned her back. "I thought if you were naked, I stood a better chance of keeping you in bed!" Sarah winced, not completely sure that she liked the way that sounded. She ignored Devlin's amused reaction.

"Sarah…" Devlin drawled out the name.

Sarah pulled clean clothes for herself from a large chest of drawers when a shiver ran through her upon hearing her name roll off Devlin's tongue that way. She slowly turned, afraid she might see Devlin standing naked behind her. Of course, from somewhere deep inside, from a place that wouldn't even admit she felt that way, Sarah also was desperately afraid she wouldn't.

The medicine began to work its magic, allowing Devlin to lean up painlessly on one elbow, the blanket slipping off one shoulder. One eyebrow arched under ebony bangs in a familiar combination of intimidation and seduction.

"Sarah, do you really think if I wanted to get up out of this bed being naked would stop me?" Devlin asked, lowering her voice an octave.

Sarah opened her mouth to speak, but no sound came out. Her face turned red and she turned away. Devlin lay down, wearing a smug smile of satisfaction. She wasn't positive, but she thought that Sarah certainly looked as though the visual image of a naked Devlin was having some sort of an effect.

A knock on the door saved both women from having to continue the conversation.

"Come in," Sarah called out.

"Got your water, Mom." Matthew came through the door with a bucket in each hand.

"Son, you are a complete godsend! Every muscle in my body needs this!"

Sarah walked to the far end of the large bedroom and pulled back the heavy curtains, which led to a small alcove. From where she lay, Devlin saw a large porcelain and brass bathing tub. Matthew emptied the buckets of water into the tub as Sarah poured a small amount of liquid from a fancy decanter into the steaming water. The fresh scent of sandalwood filled the room.

Devlin let out a low whistle. "I haven't seen a tub like that since…" She faltered, halting in mid-sentence.

Sarah had her back to Devlin, effectively hiding her smile. The only other place within a hundred miles that had a tub like this was in town at Ellen's place and Sarah knew it. She didn't smile because Devlin had visited Ellen's establishment. Sarah smiled because Devlin had stopped herself, obviously embarrassed at what Sarah's reaction would be to such knowledge. *Oh, Dev…if you only knew.*

Sarah's smile disappeared when she thought of Devlin experiencing the favors of the girls at Ellen's place. Did Devlin kiss them, touch them as she had Sarah the previous night? Sarah didn't understand what she was experiencing, but it felt a lot like…jealousy. She shook the silly notion from her head.

Matt poured the last bucket in and turned. He grinned at Devlin as he left to get more water. Devlin took in the large bruise Matthew sported over his right eye.

"How'd he get that shiner?" Dev asked once Matt had left the room.

Sarah didn't want to make Devlin feel any worse, but she didn't want to lie, either. "He held you down last night when I took the bullet out of you."

A look of pain settled on Devlin's face, and she quietly watched as the boy made a half-dozen more trips before he filled the tub. He started to leave the room, but Dev called him back.

"Matt?" She had never used his name before, and it sounded rather strange, almost formal. "Pull up a seat."

He turned over the bucket in his hand and sat next to the

bed. She stared at the boy, unsure of how to begin. "I got a kick like a mule, don't I?" She gave him a lopsided grin and the boy smiled back, gingerly rubbing the area of the bruise.

"Sure do. Never knew a woman could be that strong. You gonna be okay?"

"Yep. Takes more'n one bullet to stop me." Devlin sat with Matt for a few more minutes giving him instructions on which herd to pull in where. She also asked him to ride to his great-uncle's ranch, giving him explicit orders on what to tell Mr. Winston and requesting Hank's help in bringing in the lost herd.

Once Matthew left, Devlin realized her eyes felt like lead and she could barely keep them open. Sarah came into the room with fresh bandages, and Devlin knew it wasn't going to be good news.

"I want to take a look at your wound and change the bandages." Sarah sat on the edge of the bed next to Devlin.

"It's okay, I can do it." Devlin tried to stifle a yawn.

Sarah didn't want to embarrass either of them further, so she lifted the blanket at the middle of Devlin's body, leaving most of her body covered, except for the spot of the injury.

Devlin tried to grasp Sarah's hand to stop her progress, but her muscles went weak as she fought against the medicine.

"You waited till now 'cause you knew I'd be too tired to fight you, didn't you?" Devlin asked.

"Yep."

"You are a sneaky, devilish woman. You remind me of me." Devlin's eyes closed wearily, but a broad smile stretched across her face.

Sarah removed the old bandages to examine the wound. The area was still red and swollen, but she couldn't tell if it was because of the trauma of the surgery or an infection. Just when Sarah thought Devlin had fallen asleep, she heard a sharp intake of breath.

"I'm sorry if this hurts," Sarah said.

Devlin suddenly had trouble with the proximity of Sarah's

hands. Sarah had changed the cloth bandages, resting her hand lightly on the flat hollow of skin where Devlin's leg met her abdomen.

"You still have a slight fever," Sarah said. "Your skin still feels pretty warm."

You're telling me, Devlin thought inside her sleep-fogged brain, hoping she hadn't said it aloud. Closing her eyes tighter, Devlin fought against the pleasure of Sarah's hands attending to her just inches away from where she desperately wanted Sarah's hands to be attending to her. Devlin bit her lip until Sarah pulled the blanket back over her.

Sarah offered a sip of water and gently brushed the hair off Devlin's face.

Devlin took Sarah's free hand in her own and held it. "Sarah, you saved my life last night, thank you."

Sarah continued to stroke Devlin's forehead. "I guess that makes us even then."

"Hmm?" Dev asked, her eyes closed, enjoying Sarah's gentle touch.

"You saved my life the day you rode onto this ranch. Get some sleep now." Sarah started to move away, but Devlin's fingers tightened, drawing her back.

Sarah smiled. "Want me to stay till you fall asleep?" She renewed her caresses on Devlin's face and brow.

Nodding, Devlin felt herself slipping away as she delighted in the gentle touch of Sarah's hands. Devlin knew she didn't deserve such kindness, but the medicine had lowered her reserve enough for her to ask for the soothing contact. She couldn't remember if it was reality or a dream when she felt cool lips press softly against her forehead and murmur sweet words of comfort.

Chapter Six

Devlin ran a fever on and off for the next three days, delaying the healing process. Sarah cared for her during the entire time, feeding, bathing, and offering strong arms to hold her. Sarah knew that if Devlin had been completely aware, she would have never let Sarah hold her as she did. As it turned out, during the times when Devlin thrashed about in a fever, the only thing that could calm her was when Sarah opened her arms, Devlin snuggling into the caring embrace.

Days passed in that fashion. Sarah tended to Devlin, while Matt and Hank tended to the ranch. Eventually, Devlin's fever abated and she began the slow process of healing. She slept a great deal and still hadn't built her strength up to the point where she could argue with Sarah about anything; Sarah always won.

One afternoon, Hannah stomped into the bedroom. Devlin opened one eye to look down at her. The girl wore only her cotton slip and a pout, her small arms folded against her chest.

Dev couldn't help the smile that found its way to her face. "What's this all about, princess?"

"I hate naps!"

"Me too," Devlin agreed just as Sarah entered the room.

"Hannah Marie, what are you doing in here?" Sarah asked.

Devlin knew little about children, but she did know that they could be some of the best liars and the fastest thinkers around. Without batting an eye, Hannah jumped onto the covers with Devlin, curling herself in a ball in the crook of Devlin's arm.

"Devlin wanted me to take a nap with her."

"Oh, she did, did she?" Sarah looked at her daughter, then at Devlin, who gestured to let the girl stay.

Sarah laid a hand on Devlin's forehead, happy that she was cool to the touch and her eyes no longer held their fever-induced glaze.

"Am I all better, Mom?" Devlin's sarcasm was not lost on Sarah.

"Very funny."

"Do me a favor and load my guns." Devlin indicated the pistols that Sarah kept on the bedside table, close to Devlin.

"What for?"

"Because if you don't let me up soon, to at least go to the outhouse by myself, instead of using that thing…" Devlin indicated the chamber pot, which sat on the floor. She covered Hannah's ears with both hands. "…I'm going to shoot myself!"

Sarah simply laughed.

"All right then, ladies, get some sleep," Sarah said quietly, pulling the curtains to darken the room.

Sarah heard riders outside and watched Hank and Matt dismount.

"Good to see you again, Mrs. Tolliver," Hank said, extending his hand.

"You too, Mr. Sutton." Sarah returned the handshake. "Thank you for helping around the place and for helping Matt to bring that herd in."

"Well, I figured out pretty quick that Matt here could have done it by himself, but I was glad to oblige. I figure he must have had a good teacher."

They both knew he referred to Devlin.

"How's Dev doing?" he asked.

Sarah recognized concern on his face. "She had a pretty rough time for a while fighting off an infection, but I think all she has to do now is let her body heal. That is provided I can force her to rest any longer." Sarah laughed.

Hank joined Sarah's laughter, realizing she had an uphill battle caring for his friend.

"Keepin' her down's kinda like climbin' a greased pole, huh?" He grinned.

"Why don't we take a peek and see if she's awake? I know she wants to talk to you about what happened."

Sarah walked inside and moved toward the bedroom, Hank following behind. Sarah quietly opened the bedroom door and the sight touched her heart like no other. Devlin lay on her back, her long body stretched across the large bed, sound asleep. Her head on Devlin's shoulder, Hannah curled herself into a ball. Devlin had wrapped her arm protectively around the girl.

Sarah and Hank exchanged glances and backed out of the room without a sound. Neither of them spoke again until they were outside of the house.

"Well, guess if I didn't see that with my own eyes, I wouldn't have believed it," Hank said. "Probably best if you don't tell Dev I saw her that way, if ya know what I mean."

Sarah smiled back at Hank. "I agree. It seems that allowing others to see her vulnerabilities isn't high on her list of skills."

Hank pulled the reins over his horse's neck and prepared to mount before reaching out to shake Sarah's hand. "You're a special woman, Mrs. Tolliver. Don't bother arguing with me. We both know that Dev wouldn't let just anybody take care of her. This is only the third time in her life I've ever known her to accept help. That kind of trust don't come easy to her."

"She told me about her time with the Choctaw, and of course there's now. When was the third?"

"That's when she and I met." Hank then told the story of how he met and cared for the wounded outlaw. He left out the part about why Devlin's own men had attacked her. He didn't feel completely comfortable talking about his friend without her knowledge. He did tell Sarah how much he had come to care for Devlin after that.

"You two became…lovers then?" Sarah asked, not really understanding why she felt such trepidation in hearing the answer, also knowing it was none of her business.

Hank watched Sarah's face, and he knew. Perhaps it was the way Sarah lowered her head as she waited for his answer or the way her eyes turned just a little greener.

"No, ma'am," Hank said. Then he decided to put his trust in this woman. If Devlin trusted her, then she had the best recommendation that money could buy. "Dev's not exactly my type."

"Not your type? A beautiful, strong woman? Not your type?" Sarah asked in astonishment.

"Well, you see…the key word there is woman," Hank said, hoping Sarah would understand without him having to explain.

"Oh," Sarah said, not really understanding. She and Hank just stared at each other for a long moment.

"Oh!" Full realization finally hit her. Sarah smiled at Hank. She had heard of such relationships before but had never understood the attraction. Of course, Sarah wanted to put Hank at ease, but she also felt something else because of Hank's personal revelation. Sarah didn't understand why, but it made her happy to hear that Devlin and Hank weren't involved that way.

"Course, I'd be real obliged if you weren't to pass that on, Mrs. Tolliver, especially to your uncle."

Sarah grasped his hand and gave it a gentle squeeze. "I understand, please don't worry about that."

They shook hands once again, and Hank promised he would ride back at the end of the week to check up on the ranch and their patient. Sarah watched as the man rode away, then she walked past the house toward the vegetable garden. Bending down to pull some errant weeds out of the soft earth, Sarah thought about what Hank had told her.

It didn't matter to her how others lived their lives, as long as they afforded her the same consideration. Of course, it had been narrow-mindedness and ignorance that had driven her to leave Kentucky in the first place. She mulled over her reaction when she thought Devlin and Hank were involved. Wasn't it the same feeling that had tugged at her that morning, when her mind had visualized Devlin at Ellen's place? *Am I jealous?*

She stopped and looked up from her task, pondering the words. *No, no, no. This isn't happening.* Then Sarah remembered the touch of Devlin's breast, the way the small area of hardened flesh felt under her fingertips. The memory was enough to cause a heat to envelop her body that had little to do with the afternoon sun.

Then there was the necklace. Ever since she had put the stone around her neck, she had indeed been having the most vivid dreams. Devlin had told her about the Choctaw belief that if Sarah received the *okchako-talia* as a gift, she would dream of her heart's desire. Every night since then, Sarah had dreamed of the beautiful Devlin. Some of the dreams had been quite innocent, but most ended just before Devlin would touch Sarah the way she had always desired a lover to touch her.

Sarah wasn't completely naïve, but she didn't know if what she had dreamed of was possible between two women. She replayed Devlin's whispered words over again. *Oh, God, woman, I want you.* Evidently, Devlin thought enjoying that kind of pleasure with another woman was very possible.

Then she remembered the kiss.

Sarah walked around the back of the house and washed her face and hands from the rain barrel. She wiped them dry on the coarse towel she had set there earlier.

Sarah, come to your senses. This is another woman we're talking about here and she's your friend! She's trying just as hard as you to ride away from her past. Oh, God, am I thinking with my body here? Yes, she obviously enjoys women in her bed, but you don't. Do you?

This is ridiculous! She doesn't want you that way, Even if she did like women and she did kiss you, it was only because she was drunk. She didn't even remember doing it the next morning or she would have said something about it, at the least she would have apologized. Let's face it, a widow with two children is hardly the type for a six-foot-tall, dark-haired, blue-eyed wrangler.

Tears filled Sarah's eyes, spilling onto her cheeks. She rushed away from the house and stood alone on the prairie as sobs shook her small frame, leaving her spent and shaking. *I might as well face it. If I'm waiting for an ex-outlaw to give me her heart, I'm going to be alone for a very long time.*

When Sarah returned to the house, she silently made her way into the bedroom. Hannah and Devlin still lay sleeping on the bed, Devlin having kicked most of the blankets from her legs. Sarah splashed cool water on her face, then turned to replace the covers onto the sleeping pair.

Devlin slept in a pale blue shirt Sarah provided from the chest of clothes she had given to her on Devlin's first day at the ranch. Sarah took in the long legs and muscular thighs before she re-covered them with a blanket. She tried to fight against more tears that were just beneath the surface. Suddenly, a hand gripped her own. Sarah looked up into the sleepy eyes of Devlin.

"Are you playing mom again?" Devlin teased, whispering so as not to wake Hannah.

"Yes." Sarah smiled back.

Devlin noticed Sarah's red, puffy eyes. It was obvious the woman had been crying, but Devlin had no idea why. It broke her heart to see Sarah unhappy. "Are you all right?" she asked, pulling Sarah down until she sat on the bed.

"Yes," she replied softly. "I guess I just get like this sometimes. I'm all right, really."

Sarah caressed her sleeping daughter's face, the youngster turning and snuggling into her mother's warm embrace. Sarah gently rocked the child until she was certain the girl had drifted off again.

Devlin watched the woman and thought that she'd never seen anything as loving as the way Sarah held her child. *You hold Hannah, you held me when I had a fever, didn't you? Who holds you?*

As with most things in her life, the things she didn't think about, the impulses she acted on without thinking of the consequences usually turned out to be the best. Acting on her heart's desire alone, Devlin wrapped two strong arms around Sarah and tenderly pulled her against her chest. Devlin never felt any hesitation as Sarah let the heartfelt embrace envelop her.

Devlin's shoulder under her head felt so good to Sarah, she could feel the nerves that had been strung taut by the day's emotions start to let go and relax. Hannah wriggled herself until she lay in the laps of both women, a soft snore coming from her parted lips. Sarah and Devlin looked at each other and had to stifle their laughter.

"This girl could sleep through a twister! And if you even think about saying she takes after her mother, I'll shoot you myself, Devlin Brown!" Sarah whispered.

Sarah let herself relax in Devlin's arms. Devlin's hand stroked her hair, producing a calming effect until Sarah slept as soundly as her daughter did.

Devlin hated the fact that it took Sarah's sadness to be able to hold Sarah in her arms. Devlin burrowed her face into the sweet smell of Sarah's soft hair. *I've never been in love before. Is this what it feels like? I never wanted to give anything to anyone. I only knew how to take, but with you, it's so different. I feel guilty taking, when all I want to do is give to you. Happiness, pleasure, love, only for you, Sarah.*

Sarah slept deeply and the tiny snore that sounded like Hannah's caused Devlin to smile against Sarah's hair. Looking down into the beautiful face, Devlin felt herself losing the battle to kiss the lips of the desirable woman in her arms. She carefully leaned in and brushed her lips against Sarah's soft, full ones. A tear escaped from Devlin's eye as she realized that Sarah only considered her a friend, even more that the stolen kiss would be the only one they would ever share.

I might as well face it. If I'm waiting for a lady like this to give me her heart, I'm going to be alone for a very long time.

The healing process had begun, but the combination of having a bullet in her side and fighting off an infection for a week had left Devlin sore and physically drained. Earlier in the day, Sarah had Matthew fill the brass tub and Devlin had bathed for the first time in she didn't remember how long. It felt good to be clean and put on fresh clothes, but Devlin hated to admit that she needed Sarah's help to get her boots on. She relented, even leaning heavily on Sarah as she took her first steps out into the next room.

Devlin fidgeted in her chair as she tried to find a comfortable position. Hannah sat on the floor, a slate and a piece of chalk in her hand. She smiled up at Devlin brightly. Dev could never keep a smile off her face when Hannah was around. Matthew sat at the table, a similar slate filled with sums in front of him.

"Are you going to school, too, Dev?" Hannah asked. "I'm learning to read."

Sarah noticed a strange look pass across Devlin's face, a look bordering on panic. She dismissed it as a look of pain, noting the way Devlin fidgeted in her chair.

"Hannah, pay attention to what you're doing and let Dev rest," Sarah said.

"I thought maybe Dev wants to learn to read, too." Hannah looked up at her mother.

"Don't be silly," Matthew said. "Grownups already know how to read."

"Matthew, please don't call your sister silly. Now both of you get back to work."

Sarah was going to roll her eyes in a "why me?" gesture at Devlin, but Devlin had her head bowed, staring at her boots. Her knuckles turned white, gripping the arms of the chair. At first, Sarah thought Devlin had experienced a wave of pain, but Devlin ran her hands through her dark hair and looked up into Sarah's eyes.

Devlin gave a small smile, but it wasn't the smile Devlin usually reserved for Sarah. She thought it looked like a smile filled with apology, and she saw a touch of pain in those blue eyes. When the truth dawned on Sarah, she only wished she could do something to make Devlin feel more at ease. The only thing to do would be to create the kind of environment where Devlin would feel comfortable asking for help.

Nearly an hour went by and Matthew still had problems with the sums he worked over.

"No, honey, look..." Sarah indicated the problem on a large slate of her own. "This number is multiplied by this number."

"I can't do it!" Matt threw down his chalk in frustration. "There's too many numbers! Who knows what five hundred multiplied by three hundred twenty-five is anyway."

"One hundred sixty-two thousand, five hundred," Devlin said in a flash.

Everyone looked up at Devlin, and she sank lower in her chair.

"Hey, do it again, Dev," Matt said.

Sarah gave Devlin some more problems, and she solved them in her head within seconds. Sarah barely had time to write the entire figure on the slate before Devlin had the answer. Devlin would tap her thumb against her fingers and come up with the answer.

"That is absolutely amazing. Is it a trick?" Sarah asked.

"Kind of," she said, appearing flattered and embarrassed at the same time. "A ways back, I rode with a fella who ran a traveling medicine show. He taught me how to do it."

"Can you teach me?" Matthew asked. "Can she, Mom?"

"It's not really learnin' when you do it my way, Matt," Devlin said.

"Nonsense. Of course it's learning," Sarah interjected. "I'd rather Matt learns to do it your way and get it right than spend day after day doing it my way and never grasping it. That is, provided you want to teach us." Sarah smiled as she included herself.

Devlin smiled her usual smile, amazed that she would know something about schooling that she could teach them. "Okay, here's how you do it."

They worked for most of the day learning Devlin's number system. Even Hannah easily grasped the concept. After they had all gone off to do their individual chores, Devlin had dozed off. The next thing she knew, Sarah woke her for dinner. It was a testament to how safe and relaxed Devlin felt that she was able to sleep without leaving one eye open. She prayed to the spirits that no trouble would pass their way until she was physically able to protect Sarah and the children. Devlin smiled to herself at how Sarah would glare at her if she knew Devlin thought about her as something to protect.

Devlin couldn't remember being so tired in such a long time. Sarah came over to help Devlin out of her chair, and she had to lean on Sarah heavily so as not to put too much weight on her injured side. It wasn't only to keep her stitches from pulling loose. Earlier, when Devlin had tried to stand by herself, she nearly dropped to one knee from the pain. "Guess every year older I get, it makes it a little harder to come back from this kind of stuff," she said. "It ain't like this is the first time I been filled with lead and sewed back up."

"Let's just hope it's the last," Sarah said. "No making it like an anniversary kind of thing. I mean, I don't want to do this again every year for the next fifty. My nerves couldn't handle it."

They walked into the bedroom, and Devlin wondered if Sarah had really meant what she just said or if it had only been an expression. Sarah's words had made it sound as though she planned on Devlin hanging around for quite some time.

"Sarah, I can go out to the bunkhouse. I don't want you to have to sleep with Hannah anymore."

"You can barely walk by yourself. What if something happened and you needed help in the middle of the night? I'd never know. Besides, I wouldn't get a wink of sleep all night, even in this big comfortable bed because I'd be worrying about you."

Sarah assisted in lowering Devlin's body onto the edge of the bed. "You're going to get up and bolt the minute I turn my back, aren't you?"

"Well...bolt might be asking a lot, but I bet I could crawl pretty good."

"You're such a sensible woman. Be sensible now, not noble. Please, for me? Please?"

The plea snared Devlin. Devlin nodded, and Sarah left her with a few moments of privacy to undress.

When Sarah returned, Devlin had already changed into the shirt she usually slept in and slipped under the covers of the large four-poster bed. Sarah wore a nightgown and a cotton robe over it, tied at the waist. She sat at the small vanity and began to pull the braids from her hair. Sarah usually kept the front strands of her long hair braided and pulled back to keep it off her face, letting the mane at the back of her head fall free.

Devlin thought that there was no more beautiful sight on Earth as the one she watched just then. Sarah slowly ran a brush through long locks. When she rose, she walked over and sat on the edge of the bed, tucking her slim legs underneath her.

"Did you want me to read tonight?" She reached for a book that she kept on the bedside table. While Devlin had been confined to a bed, Sarah had made a habit of reading to her from *The Count of Monte Cristo*. Devlin enjoyed the story immensely, but that night, she shook her head sadly.

"You don't have to read to me."

"I know I don't have to, but...I'm sorry, you should have said something sooner. I thought you were enjoying the story."

"No...it's not that, it's just..." Devlin took the book from Sarah's grasp, returning it to the bedside table. "What I mean is you don't *have* to read to me." Devlin leaned her head back and closed her eyes, unwilling to meet Sarah's questioning gaze.

"You'll finish it yourself then?"

Devlin opened her eyes, which suddenly filled with tears. When the tears began to spill onto her cheeks, she raised her eyes to the ceiling, willing the tears to stop.

"I think we both know that's not going to happen," Dev said, realizing that Sarah already knew her secret.

"Dev, I could he—"

"No. Sarah, please…don't." Dev cursed herself because the tears now fell in earnest, and it seemed she could do nothing to stop them. She couldn't even run away. "I don't want pity or charity, especially from you."

"Is that why you think I want to help you? Out of pity?" Sarah reached up to brush the tears from Devlin's face.

Devlin brusquely turned her head away from Sarah's touch, unable to control her feelings of frustration.

"I didn't offer to help you because I felt sorry for you. I did it because that's what you do for someone when you care about them, when they're as close to you as…as your own sister. When you love someone as much as your own family, you offer to help whatever their need. I know it must be embarrassing, not to mention frustrating for you. I just wanted to be able to help, not make you feel worse." When Sarah finished, she had tears in her eyes.

"I'm sorry. I just get…I haven't cried since I was seven." The admission brought back a long buried memory for Devlin. In a shaky voice, she told Sarah the story. "The last time I cried was the day they brought my father's body home."

His six-foot-six-inch frame lay across a door as they carried him into the parlor. One bullet to his chest had been enough to take the lawman down. Dev remembered one of her father's deputies lifting her up in his arms and telling her what a hero the sheriff had been. That day, she cried for her father, the man she adored. It was the last day that Devlin ever remembered crying.

Devlin could barely hold back the sobs that she desperately tried to catch in her throat. Sarah leaned back against the headboard of the bed and didn't have to ask twice before Devlin fell into her embrace. Sarah's heart broke for the woman who had found herself unable to cry all those years.

Sarah whispered against Devlin's temple. "Please, you don't have to be afraid of being yourself in front of me. When you care about someone, you love all of them, the good, the bad, and everything in between."

The feel of Sarah's lips against her skin and the strong, loving embrace finally tore through what small defenses Devlin had left. Devlin let her heart-breaking sobs loose, and Sarah held her, all the while whispering tender words of comfort and friendship to the distressed woman.

Nearly an hour passed before Devlin had no tears left to cry. Still she lay in Sarah's embrace, enjoying the closeness along with Sarah's caress. Sarah reached into the bedside table and produced a handkerchief that she handed to Devlin.

"Thanks," Devlin said, sitting up against the headboard. "I don't know what came over me."

"I bet you feel better." Sarah stood and wet a cloth from a pitcher on the vanity.

"Actually, I do," Dev admitted with a sheepish grin.

Sarah handed the cool fabric to Devlin and she wiped her face. Once Sarah sat on the bed again, Devlin reached past her to pick up the book that still lay unopened on the bed. She handed it to Sarah.

"Can you teach me? I mean, I know enough to get me by, but…can you teach me to read the kind of words that are in this book?" Devlin was afraid to look Sarah in the eye. Mustering her courage, she raised her head and looked into warm green eyes.

Sarah smiled and nodded.

"Can we start now?" Devlin asked with a tone of hesitancy

in her voice.

Sarah was so tired and she knew that Devlin must be doubly exhausted, but she didn't want to take the chance that Devlin might think twice about the whole thing by morning. Again, Sarah nodded.

"Your feet must be freezing. Here." Devlin pulled the comforter back and wrapped it around Sarah.

Sparks of desire snapped around each woman at the proximity of the other, but throughout all the powerful emotions, Devlin and Sarah knew that they had each found a lifelong friend. So they pushed the stronger feelings down and snuggled under the covers like two schoolgirls.

The next morning, Sarah woke with a start when Hannah jumped onto her stomach.

"Mama, I'm hungry," the youngster whispered.

Sarah still had her eyes closed. "Hannah, why are you whispering?"

For some reason, Sarah found herself whispering back. When she opened her eyes, Hannah had her pudgy fingers held up to pursed lips, motioning for her mother to be quiet, then pointed next to them. Devlin's still sleeping figure lay curled up against Sarah's side. Sarah was afraid to move. Her daughter smiled down at Devlin as if it was the most natural thing in the world for her mother to be sharing her bed with Devlin.

"Hannah," Sarah whispered, attempting to slide her body off the bed.

The six-year-old couldn't resist poking out her index finger and touching Devlin's lips. Just as she neared Devlin's mouth, Devlin's white teeth gleamed in a huge crocodile-like grin, and with her eyes still closed, Devlin snapped her teeth loudly at the offending finger.

Devlin knew how far away Hannah's finger was, and she had no intention of biting the girl, but the youngster certainly didn't know that. Hannah jumped back with a scream and plenty of giggles, right into her mother, who was still in the process of easing herself out of bed.

Thirty pounds of squealing, laughing child came rushing at Sarah. The force of the impact caused her to lose her balance, tossing her off the bed. Devlin reached out and caught Hannah, keeping the girl from landing on top of Sarah.

Sarah landed on her back and leaned up on both elbows as two heads peeked over the edge of the bed. Devlin and Hannah looked at each other.

"See what you made me do," they said in unison, followed by their own loud laughter.

Sarah picked herself up off the floor and glared at both her bedmates. They tried to hide their smiles at her predicament.

"You two wear me out. You definitely wear me out." She picked up her pillow and sailed it at the two heads that ducked the object easily.

Sarah rose and prepared to leave the room to make breakfast, still shaking her head in exasperation. She stopped to watch Devlin tickle Hannah's ears, the girl resuming her peals of laughter. The moment would live forever in her memory. Sarah couldn't ever remember being as happy as she felt just then.

Devlin watched Sarah walk from the room, resuming her attack on the girl. Finally, Hannah tired herself out and fell silent in Devlin's embrace. Devlin rocked Hannah and began to hum a tune that she remembered from her childhood.

Devlin's eye caught the book, which Sarah had placed on the bedside table and her memory took her to the night before. Each of them had fallen asleep while reading. They pushed the book aside and unconsciously snuggled together in sleep. Devlin remembered waking in the middle of the night, feeling Sarah's warm body and deep, even breathing. Just the feel of Sarah's body comforted Devlin. Slipping her arm around Sarah's waist, Devlin felt Sarah unconsciously press her back against her chest.

She remembered Sarah saying that she loved her. Sarah had explained that Devlin was as close as family, and on some level, that was more than Devlin had ever dared hope for.

"I guess that means you're my family now, too, princess," Devlin said, kissing the top of Hannah's head.

By the time the cool winds of fall swept across the Oklahoma prairie, Devlin had finished *The Count of Monte Cristo*. Except this time, Devlin read to Sarah every evening.

Chapter Seven

Devlin had recuperated fully from her bullet wound, once again riding herd for the Double Deuce. Her injury and the time she had spent with Sarah and the children had changed her somewhat. She was no longer the mysterious stranger the Tollivers were in awe over. Now Devlin was a part of the family. She came in from the range at night and enjoyed dinner with the family, taking the time to give Matt a math lesson and tell Hannah a bedtime story. She always finished Hannah's story by lifting the youngster high into the air, scooping her into strong arms, and placing a kiss on the top of her head.

After the children had gone to sleep, Devlin and Sarah usually spent their evenings talking in low voices, sitting by the fireplace, or listening to Devlin read aloud from their latest literary choice. They were in the middle of *Treasure Island*. Devlin loved the pirates in the story. Occasionally, Sarah fell asleep by the fire as Devlin read. Sarah enjoyed listening to the rich, low tone of her friend's voice, sometimes becoming so relaxed that she drifted off into a heavy sleep. Those were the times Devlin would gently lift Sarah into her arms and carry her into the bedroom, tucking her under the covers. Then Devlin would go around the back of the house to her own large room, usually to spend the rest of the night thinking about the woman on the other side of the wall.

The sun shone brightly, but the cool October breeze blew down from the north, adding a touch of color to Sarah's cheeks. They started the day with a trip to town, setting out just after the sun had risen to get an early start on the long ride. The cold never seemed to affect Devlin, but she had thrown her leather jacket over the front bench of the wagon just in case. Matthew and Hannah rode in the back as Devlin held the reins of the old buckboard. Sarah sat next to Devlin.

"I sure hope Alexander knows how to ride when he gets here. He could come out and ride herd with me," Matthew said excitedly.

"Your Aunt Mattie is going to be here for a month, Matthew. I'm sure there will be plenty of time for you to teach your cousin if he doesn't already know how," Sarah said, looking at her son.

Devlin listened while Sarah answered her children's questions about their aunt and the cousins they hadn't seen in years. Sarah then entertained the children with stories about her sister Madeline and all the trouble they managed to get into on their Kentucky farm. Some time later, Sarah looked over at Devlin next to her.

"What are you smiling about today?" Sarah noticed the grin on Devlin's face at breakfast and had watched it come and go all morning, usually reappearing when Devlin thought no one was watching.

"Can't I be in a good mood every once in a while?" Devlin asked, not taking her eyes off the dirt road.

"Sure," Sarah said. "And that would make this…what, the second time in how many years?"

Devlin looked at Sarah, arching an eyebrow and growling under her breath. Sarah was neither intimidated nor frightened by the ex-outlaw's infamous look. Sarah laughed and pulled the brim of Devlin's hat down over her eyes.

Sarah and Devlin enjoyed their playful exchanges, but each secretly longed for so much more. Neither was willing to take any measures to elevate the relationship further. Without the other realizing it, they each feared losing the precious friendship that had developed over the past six months.

Once Sarah began talking to the children again, Devlin's

secretive smile returned. Devlin's heart felt lighter than it ever had before. The previous evening, she had admitted to herself that she was in love with Sarah. She felt like a woman who had suffered from a fever for the past six months, only to have the sickness break. Her body was still weak but well on the way to recovery. Only the night before, Devlin had put her remaining fears to rest regarding her unrequited passion for Sarah.

Devlin's newfound reading skills came in handy once she started finding the tumbleweed notes again, but she experienced conflicting emotions when it came to the mysterious woman who had written the notes. For so long, Devlin had pined away for the mystifying, heartbroken woman. She had fallen hard for Sarah, but she couldn't explain why she still felt some sort of pull to the emotional outpourings of the stranger. It began to concern Devlin, questioning herself and whether she was truly in love with Sarah. It had been so long since Devlin had felt anything remotely similar to love that she had begun to doubt her own heart. The night before sealed not only her love for Sarah, but also her destiny. The day had started out as any other...

Hank had an evening off and rode out to the Double Deuce to see if Devlin wanted to make the trek into town for the evening; Hank had an itch to play cards. Of course, Hank had a feeling his friend would turn him down. Devlin made up an excuse about being too tired to chase skirts and having to get up at dawn to make a trip to town, but Hank understood. It seemed as if other women suddenly lost their appeal to Devlin, and when Sarah came outside to invite him to stay for dinner, he certainly understood why his friend felt the way she did.

"You look happy and kinda sick at the same time, Dev. What's got ya down?" Hank asked as if he didn't know.

"I got something burnin' me up from the inside out, Hank," Devlin said, looking back to the cabin.

"You got tumbleweed fever is all." Hank slapped her on the back.

"What?" Dev turned to face Hank. She couldn't believe he knew.

"Close your mouth and don't look so surprised. Half the cowhands in the territory are passin' around those little pieces of parchment. Some gal got it into her mind to torment the wranglers and she's doin' a good job, too. If you went to Ellen's anymore, you'd know they got a huge pool goin' about what the gal looks like…thin and tall, short and fat. Hell, chances are she's an eighty-two-year-old widow!"

Devlin just continued to stare at her friend. He looked her in the eye and decided to push matters a little.

"Look, Dev, you got a good thing here, someone special in that girl." He motioned with his head toward the cabin. "Don't mess it up by dreamin' you could ever find better 'n her."

Devlin looked out into the darkness. Running her fingers through her hair, she then replaced her hat and pulled it firmly onto her head. She felt an ache in her gut as she prepared to say the words aloud for the first time.

"She doesn't belong to me. She'll never belong to me that way."

Hank shook his head and grinned. "Then you're the only one who don't know it."

"You really think so?"

Hank leaned back his head and laughed.

Devlin found her friend's humor infectious, even if it was at her expense. She punched him in the arm and pulled him toward the house. "If you think she's special now, just wait till you taste her biscuits."

During dinner, Hank watched the way Devlin interacted with Sarah and her children. He could hardly believe she was the same woman he had known for the past year. She smiled and let Sarah tease her, retaliating with some of her own good-natured jibes. It was as if they were a real family. Then again, he also enjoyed watching the two women watch each other when they thought no one was looking. It made his heart glad *t*o see his usually taciturn friend happy and content. The only female he couldn't get to take to him was Hannah.

The youngster stayed as far away from him as possible. She clung to her mother's skirts through most of the evening or sat in Sarah's lap, eyeing the stranger warily. When Sarah got up to serve dessert, Hank and Dev stood as Sarah left the table. When Hank looked down at the child and grinned at her, she sped right past her mother and much to everyone's surprise, leapt into Devlin's lap. No amount of coaxing could talk the child into leaving the safety of the lap as she buried her head into Devlin's shoulder. Hank was amazed at how comfortable Devlin appeared with her arms wrapped around the youngster.

Later, Devlin and Sarah sat outside, even though the night air had a chill to it. Devlin surprised Sarah by bringing out two steaming cups of coffee. Then Devlin wrapped her leather coat around Sarah's shoulders.

"I'm surprised you didn't want something with more of a bite to it than this," Sarah said with a smile.

"Oh, this will keep you plenty warm." Devlin grinned back.

Sarah swallowed a sip of the hot liquid and exhaled a warm puff of air from her mouth. Devlin had taken her by surprise, as Sarah felt the whiskey already begin to warm her through.

"Yeah, you're right." She laughed at Devlin, who rolled her eyes and whistled, feigning innocence.

The two talked as they always did, openly and honestly about anything that came to mind. Devlin's mind wandered as she watched Sarah speak, but something she heard jerked her back into the present.

"What did you say?" Devlin asked, certain she hadn't heard Sarah correctly.

"I said I love being able to just sit here, staring at the stars. I love this place, Dev, this land. All that my heart desires is right here, all around me, everywhere I look. I'm glad I finally have someone to share it with."

Sarah watched as Devlin's eyes went wide, her pupils dilating until there was only a thin ring of clear blue left.

"I mean...I'm glad I have someone to share a beautiful night like this with," Sarah quickly added.

Devlin composed herself, but she didn't act the same the rest of the night. She listened and talked with Sarah, but her mind was a million miles away from the conversation at hand. When Devlin finally excused herself for the night, Sarah cursed herself for revealing too much of her heart, sure that's what drove Devlin to her silent behavior.

Devlin, in the meantime, couldn't get back to her room fast enough. She rifled through her meager belongings for the packet of tumbleweed notes. She pulled the ribbon away and began rifling through the collection of papers for something in particular. It was something Sarah had said. It was Devlin's custom to go back on occasion and reread the notes. Her improved reading skills put many of the notes into a new light. Devlin had heard Sarah say something, however, that she couldn't believe. It had sounded more than vaguely familiar. Here's the one, she thought to herself, pulling the note from the bundle.

No one has ever held my heart, not the way that I dream of...

Is it wrong to wish for a lover that will captivate my heart, as well as my body?

Too long have I waited for the warrior of my soul...I am thinking that I will always be alone,

All that my heart desires is right here, all around me, everywhere I look,

Still it means so little without someone to share it.

Devlin held the note out in front of her with shaking hands. The last two lines were the exact same words Sarah had said to her. She sat on the floor, her back resting against the bed, pulling notes from the packet at random. She had to be sure.

After all, it could have been mere coincidence. From every dozen or so notes she read, Devlin recognized a phrase that belonged to Sarah, something she had said.

Scenes and random snatches of conversation rushed through Devlin's mind. She pulled her hat from her head and ran her fingers through her ebony mane, her gaze staring straight ahead, unseeing. Devlin sat there as the notes, scattered in front of her, took life. She visualized Sarah speaking every word, her melodic voice whispering the secret desires of her heart. The scenes swirled around her mind like a whirlpool, spinning faster and faster until they all converged at one point.

Sarah was the author of the tumbleweed notes.

Devlin remembered Kontonalah's visit with the Indian trading party. Her grandfather told her they had named Sarah into the Thunderbird clan because Keeho had a vision. The healer had spoken of a small sakli, a salmon always trying to swim upstream, always moving against the current. The healer said they had witnessed Sarah sending messages to the spirits on the wings of the wind.

She hadn't quite known what to say to her grandfather at the time. She certainly didn't want to disrespect him or the old beliefs. Devlin laughed aloud, thinking of what they had actually seen Sarah doing. They saw her tying a note to a piece of dried sagebrush!

Devlin laughed until she cried. She had dreamed of Sarah before they'd even met. It was no wonder to her that she still felt a pull toward the author of the notes, even after she had fallen in love with Sarah. She could only wonder what her grandfather would say about the omens there.

Devlin pulled on the familiar blue shirt she had become accustomed to wearing to bed and piled her boots and clothes neatly next to the bed. One of her guns lay under her pillow; the other remained in her holster, which she had looped over the nearby poster of the bunk. Devlin blew out the kerosene lamp, lying down and crossing her hands behind her head. A sly smile played on her lips.

"Tumbleweed fever…I'll be damned," she said. "Open up your eyes and turn around, Sarah, I'm right here," she whispered in a tired voice before rolling over to dream of her heart's desire.

Devlin pulled their wagon to a stop in front of the general store, so the young men in the store could load their supplies into the buckboard. Sarah had a large number of supplies to purchase before the cold winds of winter hit. Devlin jumped down and moved to help Sarah from the front of the wagon. Devlin's hands around Sarah's slim hips caused the return of Devlin's reticent smile. It also brought a slight blush to Sarah's cheeks.

After easily lifting Hannah from the back of the wagon, Devlin followed the group into the store. Devlin hadn't been there in over a year, when she had purchased the length of green ribbon. She felt slightly uncomfortable at the memory.

"Dev, lift me up," Hannah said.

"Lift you up, what?" Devlin asked.

"Pleeeaase." Hannah smiled up at the woman.

"That's better." She lifted the girl up to look at the jars of candy on the counter.

"Which one, princess?"

Hannah pointed to a jar of hard cherry candies. Dev smiled. They were her favorite, too.

After Devlin purchased a small sack of the candies, she split them between the two children and popped one into her mouth.

"I don't care if you got the money. We don't serve your kind. Go on, git!" a man behind the dry goods counter raised his voice to a young Indian man.

It must have been the Indian's family who waited in a far corner of the store. A pretty young woman and a girl about Hannah's age stood nervously in the shadows. Sarah smiled and walked over to the young woman. Mother and child smiled back.

"*Halito*," Sarah said softly when she recognized the mark of the Thunderbird clan on the woman's leather and bead belt.

"*Halito, chim achukma?*" the woman returned the greeting.

Hannah had Devlin by the hand, pulling her over to where her mother stood. Hannah hid behind Devlin's legs and smiled shyly at the Indian girl. The youngster reached into the sack of candy Devlin had bought and pulled some out. Holding her hand out to the child, Hannah waited for the other girl to take the offered candy. The Indian girl looked afraid, but Devlin kneeled down until she was more along the height of the two youngsters and spoke to the frightened girl.

"*Halito, hachi banna?*" she said as the girl's face brightened and she plucked the candy from Hannah's palm. Both girls smiled and giggled.

"*Yakoke*," the clan girl said in thanks.

Sarah had become quite good at the language Devlin had taught her. She conversed briefly with the girl's mother until the brave stood before her, eyeing her with suspicion. He motioned with his hand for his wife to leave. Devlin stood up to her full height and glared at the man for his bad manners. Looking a little chagrined, the brave held out his arm to Devlin, who accepted it.

"*Halito, Redhawk*," he said.

After a few moments, the Choctaw family left, leaving Sarah to wonder what happened to make the brave so angry. When she questioned Devlin, Devlin whispered so no one in the store would overhear.

"They wanted to buy ten blankets. They had the money, but the clerk wouldn't sell him any."

"Because they were Indians?" Sarah asked, shocked at the clerk's behavior.

Devlin nodded. Sarah's old friend owned the store, and she was surprised that anyone who worked for Mr. Grayson would act that way. With all Devlin had told her about the Choctaw people, Sarah knew she couldn't talk the Indians into accepting the blankets from her, but she formulated a plan in her head.

Sarah walked up to the dry goods counter to the smiles of a number of the clerks. She did not live in town, but they all knew her. They also knew of the dark wrangler who stood slightly behind her, watching everything Sarah did through protective eyes. Most of them realized Sarah owned a prosperous ranch, and when it came to the laying in of winter supplies, she could make or break the store with a year's worth of purchases. Most of them knew Sarah, except for the unfortunate young man who was also about to see her temper firsthand.

"The wagon is right out front, please load this list of supplies, won't you…Donald?" Sarah asked sweetly, leaning in slightly to read the name sewn onto the young man's vest. "Oh, and would you add ten wool blankets to that list?"

The young man frowned and looked at her warily. "Who are ya buying them for?"

Sarah's eyebrow raised and her smile froze in place. She took a step closer and placed her hands on top of the counter.

Devlin had begun to enjoy herself. Upon seeing the fire in Sarah's eyes, Devlin thought someone should have warned the man.

"I beg your pardon, young man?" Sarah asked, her smile frozen in place, but with a touch of ice added to her sweet voice.

One of the girls behind the counter slipped away and returned in an instant with an older man in his fifties, who was as large around the middle as he was tall. Devlin recognized the owner of the store rushing out to intercept the possible loss of one of his best customers.

"Sarah!" He rushed to her and swept her in his arms.

Sarah couldn't help laughing at the older man; his smile was contagious, and she could feel her foul temper dissipating.

"Franklin, it's been too long, how is Marie?" Sarah asked.

"Mean as ever!" He laughed.

"I heard that, old man!" A woman as small as Sarah rushed from the backroom and threw her arms around Sarah. "You're as pretty as ever," the older woman complimented. "And is this little Hannah? Why she was just a little bit of nothin' last time you were here...and Matthew. My, what a strong young man you turned out to be."

Introductions went around, then Sarah did something unexpected. "I'd like you to meet a friend of mine." Sarah looked behind her at Devlin, who suddenly realized Sarah was introducing her.

"Dev...this is Frank and Marie Grayson...this is Devlin Brown." Sarah made the introductions and watched as Frank grabbed Dev's hand immediately. Devlin looked a little shocked but remembered to remove her hat when she greeted the portly man's wife.

"Were you finding everything you need, Devlin?" Frank Grayson said in an attempt at casual conversation.

"Actually," Devlin paused to look at Sarah, "Sarah seems to be having a little trouble."

Sarah looked into the blue gaze. Then she placed a sweet smile on her face and laughed. "Frank, I didn't realize I had to justify all my purchases now. Is that a new policy?"

The shop owner looked at the clerk behind the counter. "Donald, are you having a problem filling Mrs. Tolliver's order?" Frank asked in a severe tone.

Dev thought the clerk should have known to leave well enough alone. She would have thought after seeing what close friends the Graysons were with Sarah and her family, he would have apologized and went about his business. Some men never learn, and at the rate young Donald was progressing, he wouldn't make it far into his manhood before he would infuriate someone with a set of guns around his waist.

"She was trying to buy blankets for those Indians I threw out of here earlier." Donald sneered.

Frank's eyes narrowed at the young man. "Do you mean to tell me you turned away paying customers?"

"But they were Indians," he whined.

"Donald..." Frank's face lost its naturally cordial

appearance. "Get out of my store. You're fired."

The clerk looked shocked but made no attempt to leave until Devlin shot the boy a withering glance that just about buckled his knees. He scooped up his belongings and quickly left.

"Evie, do you think you can get Mrs. Tolliver's order together for her?" Frank asked the young girl who had thought to call the storeowner in the first place.

"Yes, Mr. Grayson." She smiled at Sarah.

"There you go, little one," Frank said to Sarah with a smile, using the term of endearment that had become familiar to Sarah. "My new head clerk, Evie Sinclair, will take care of everything for you."

Evie gasped and thanked the older man before he returned to his back room, but not before he and his wife extracted a promise of dinner with Sarah and her family.

"Congratulations on your promotion, Miss Sinclair." Sarah smiled knowingly at the clerk. Sarah then took Hannah from Devlin's arms, leading the youngster back toward the bolts of fabric.

The last time Devlin had been in the store, the clerks scattered like Devlin was going to call them out for a gunfight at high noon. Since she was there with Sarah, holding Hannah in her arms, they had a chance to see what Devlin was really like. Up until that point, Dev had been a legendary outlaw, the kind of person they only read about in dime novels. Suddenly, one or two of the girls in the store realized how charming Devlin's smile was and how her eyes sparkled. They could have saved themselves some trouble if they had only bothered to see that the charming smile and sparkling eyes were only meant for one woman.

Evie watched Devlin as she checked items from Sarah's list, assigning them to the young men to load into the wagon.

"I saw you in here once before, you know," Evie said. Devlin noticed it had grown warmer in the store as the girl began to flirt shamelessly. Sarah stood not five feet away, an amused look on her face.

"You bought a piece of ribbon. Was it for your girlfriend?" Evie asked, looking curiously at Sarah.

Devlin found herself unable to speak, wishing she could go back to when they had been frightened of her. She shook her head, nervously looking over to where Sarah stood. Sarah, in the meantime, seemed to enjoy Devlin's predicament, noticing her ears had nearly turned scarlet. Smiling to herself, Sarah liked how absolutely cute Devlin looked, trying to fend off the advances of the girl.

"If you're interested, I get off work soon," Evie whispered, but not quiet enough for Sarah to miss.

A small stab of pain cut through Sarah as she eavesdropped, waiting to hear Devlin's answer.

"Sorry, darlin'." Devlin grinned, suddenly aware that Sarah had been straining to listen to the conversation. "But I'm spoken for."

Sarah was glad she had her back to Devlin because she couldn't refuse the enormous smile that spread across her face.

Their shopping complete, they walked down the wood plank sidewalk in front of the shops, Hannah skipping ahead playfully.

"How about we go into the hotel for lunch?" Sarah asked. When she received an agreement from the other three members of the group, Matthew and Hannah ran ahead.

Sarah had begun to feel extremely guilty, not only for eavesdropping on Devlin's conversation with the shop girl, but also because Devlin had probably turned Evie down because of Sarah and the children. It didn't take much more for Sarah to realize that she was absolutely in love with Devlin. The comprehension didn't bother her nearly as much as wondering why she harbored no adverse reactions to the idea of being in love with another woman. She realized, too, that she was probably the last thing on earth Devlin had in mind for a lover.

"Dev, I don't want you to think you have to babysit us all day. I heard that girl…I mean, if you want to go out with her…" Sarah couldn't bring herself to finish the thought.

Devlin watched Sarah out of the corner of her eye as she struggled to find the right words. Dev stopped walking and turned to look down at Sarah. She could only wonder at what Sarah was truly feeling.

"Sarah, look at me," Devlin commanded but not harshly.

Sarah stared up into the blue eyes, waiting to hear something she knew would break her heart. Meanwhile, Devlin thought she saw the misty glint of a tear in the jade-colored eyes. Devlin leaned in and gave her a lopsided grin. "I think my saddle is older than that girl. She's not exactly what I'm looking for."

Sarah wanted to throw her arms around Devlin's neck. She wanted to ask Devlin if she could be what Devlin wanted. Instead of saying or acting on any of her emotions, Sarah smiled. Devlin took her arm and they moved to catch up with the children in front of the hotel.

Entering the hotel's restaurant, they heard the sound of laughing male voices. Sarah noticed that her old friends from the barbecue sat around a large round table. A number of the men looked up, caught sight of Sarah and Devlin, and turned back to their table, raucous laughter filling the restaurant.

"Matthew, Hannah, come here," Sarah ordered softly. "I've changed my mind. Wouldn't some of Margie's chocolate cake be better than vegetables?" She smiled.

Both children nodded enthusiastically.

"You go on to the café and tell Margie I said for you to have a big piece of chocolate cake and a glass of milk. Dev and I will be there shortly, all right?" She pressed two coins into Matt's hand. "Hold your sister's hand, Matt."

She watched the children leave, then made her way over to the table of cattlemen, followed closely by Devlin. The silence reached a deafening crescendo once she reached their table.

"Gentlemen, don't stop laughing on my account. That is…"

She smiled like a tiger toying with its meal. "Unless you're laughing on my account."

At least a number of the men had the good manners to look embarrassed, but John Montgomery puffed on his cigar, staring daggers at Devlin and openly leering at Sarah.

"Well, Mrs. Tolliver, you might as well know it right off, what people think you're doing on that ranch with a woman, and I use that term loosely, like her." He motioned toward Devlin.

Devlin had moved closer to Sarah. She would have loved to take Montgomery out but didn't dare start a fight where Sarah might get hurt.

"Come on, Sarah." Devlin urged her to leave.

"No!" Sarah turned to face Devlin.

Devlin knew that Sarah's temper was a force as strong as any prairie twister. The calmer Sarah acted on the outside, the more she seethed on the inside. Just then, Sarah acted so calm that it scared the hell out of Devlin, and she wanted to be nowhere near the receiving end. Besides, Sarah seemed to be doing rather well, so Devlin bit the inside of her cheek and remained silent.

"Sit," Sarah ordered Devlin.

Feeling the heat radiating from Sarah's body and the slow, feral smile that spread across her lips, Devlin did what any other self-respecting man or woman would have done in her place. She immediately sat.

Once more, Sarah directed her attention back to the men at the table. "Now, Mr. Montgomery, about what I do on my ranch." She stood behind the man and bent close to his ear. "Would you like to know what goes on?" Without waiting for an answer, she whispered in his ear.

Devlin groaned to herself at the evil grin Sarah had on her face and the sudden change in the pallor of Montgomery's complexion.

Sarah stood straight up, walking to a spot at the head of the table, her hands resting on the backs of two separate chairs.

"You may not like me very much, gentlemen. Trust me, I'm not too terribly taken with any of you, either, but we are all cattle ranchers. I'm not going anywhere. I'm here to stay, so get over it."

"You could always sell. I'd be happy to offer you a fair price," Montgomery said, wearing an insincere smile.

"For the final time, you'll never get my land, John Montgomery!" Sarah said vehemently.

"Well, maybe your uncle will feel differently." He sneered.

Sarah laughed in the man's face. "My uncle would die before he gave his land up to someone like you." Sarah walked toward Devlin, her hands shaking. "Now we're ready to leave," Sarah said, moving to the door. She didn't bother to see if Devlin followed her. Sarah knew she had to get out of there before the tears that burned the back of her eyes fell.

"Yes, ma'am," Devlin said in wonderment at the woman whose size most certainly did not reflect the strength she held within. Devlin jumped up and stood in front of the angry woman, pulling open the door ahead of her. Devlin tipped her hat as Sarah passed by and through the open door.

"Oh, those...men!" Sarah said between clenched teeth as she and Devlin walked toward the café. Sarah finally took notice of Devlin's silence and it unnerved her. "Are you going to say anything at all?"

"Not on your life." Devlin's white teeth gleamed in a broad smile.

Sarah had to laugh. She and Devlin nearly fell into each other's arms, they were laughing so hard, and it felt so good after the last few moments of tension. There were too many people and wagons bustling around on the busy dirt road to take notice of the two women, so Devlin reached in to give Sarah a comforting hug.

"Well, hello there, Stretch," a female voice called out from behind Sarah.

Devlin's heart sank. *Oh, great...I'm on a train, and it's*

going straight to hell!

Sarah released herself from Devlin's light embrace to find the source of the familiar voice.

"Ellen!" Sarah said with delight.

"Sarah?" The madame looked surprised.

Devlin stared, open-mouthed, at the two women, the one she loved and the madame of the local brothel, obviously friends. *Train's stopped, all out. It's official, I'm in hell!*

The two women threw their arms around each other, and Devlin tried to blend in to the scenery. While she'd never actually enjoyed the pleasure of the madame's bed, she'd flirted with her enough to be sufficiently embarrassed.

Ellen was a good fifteen years older than Sarah was, but she still had the body of a working girl half her age. She owned a prosperous business with ten girls in her house. Ellen no longer made her living on her back, but she did entertain certain men and women when the mood struck her.

"You look absolutely wonderful," Ellen told Sarah. "I was so sorry to hear about Peter."

"Thank you." Sarah squeezed her friend's hand. "You're looking pretty relaxed yourself these days. The life of high finance must agree with you."

Hannah and Matt came running up to the women; the girl had chocolate smeared across her mouth and cheeks.

"Dev, lift me up." Hannah hopped up and down.

"Lift you up, what?" Dev asked.

"Pleeeaase." Hannah gave her a chocolate smile.

"That's better." She lifted the girl up as the youngster giggled at their recurring joke.

Sarah pulled out a hankie and wiped the mess from her daughter's face.

"Is this Hannah...and Matthew?" Ellen looked at the boy as Dev flipped a slender finger at the brim of the boy's hat. Matt pulled the hat from his head and shook hands with the woman.

"You're almost a grown man!" Ellen said.

"Oh, please, El. I've got enough trouble as it is." Sarah rolled her eyes.

"And precious Hannah. I think you were taking a nap in your crib the last time I saw you." She smiled at the youngster, who beamed back.

"I don't have ta sleep in a crib anymore. I sleep in my own bed, all by myself 'cept when I sleep with Mama and Dev."

Three pairs of adult eyes widened at the girl's words. Ellen could barely believe what she'd heard and was thinking she didn't know her friend half as well as she thought. Sarah had lost her voice completely, but her gaze was on Devlin, watching the stunned expression on her face. The youngster was apparently just picking up steam in her conversation, when Devlin slipped a hand over the girl's mouth.

"Didn't you say you wanted chocolate cake?" Devlin released her hand.

"But, Dev, I already had some."

"Let's go get some more. Come on, Matt." Dev quickly walked back toward the café, the little chatterbox still talking away in her arms.

"You could certainly do worse," Ellen said as she and Sarah watched the rapidly retreating figure of Devlin.

Sarah looked into her friend's amused face and felt the last few moments come crashing in on her. Tears formed in Sarah's eyes.

"Come on, girl, you look like you need a drink." Ellen put an arm around Sarah's shoulder and guided her in the direction of her establishment.

Sitting in a room curtained off from the front parlor, Ellen poured each of them a generous portion of Kentucky bourbon and left the bottle on the table. She sat and looked at Sarah, waiting for her to speak.

"What you heard Hannah say, that's not exactly what happened." Sarah explained how Dev had been shot and Devlin's subsequent recuperation. "We're not together like that," she finished, wiping an errant tear from her cheek.

"But you want to be, don't you?" Ellen asked gently, recognizing the pain in her face.

"I don't know how something like this could happen to me!" Sarah blurted out. "I'm a widow! I've been married...to a man. I have two children. This isn't exactly what I had planned. El, I don't understand any of the feelings I'm having for this woman. How could my heart...my body, just go and switch all the rules around like this?"

Ellen had heard the sentiment before, and she understood.

"Sarah, it's like this...most every day of your life, you have boiled potatoes with your dinner. Day in day out, those potatoes are always boiled. Then one day, out of the blue and for no apparent reason, you have your potatoes fried. Now you might eventually go back to your boiled potatoes. You might find that you like to have them both ways, and maybe, just maybe, you end up realizing that fried is the way you really wanted them all along. Remember one thing, kid..." Ellen lifted Sarah's chin. "The very best thing in this world is when you find someone who loves potatoes just the way you do."

Sarah smiled at Ellen and raised her glass. The story made a difference to Sarah. Her smile appeared easy and she had a bit of sparkle in her eye. They touched glasses, and Sarah confided in Ellen all that had transpired over the past six months.

Devlin walked along the sidewalk with Hannah and Matthew. She had watched Ellen and Sarah from the café window, completely surprised when she saw the two walk into Ellen's place.

"Matt, you stay here and watch your sister. I'm going to get your mother. We won't be too long."

"But I want to go in, too," Matt pleaded. Pulling himself up to his full height, he tried to make his voice deeper, to Devlin's amusement. "I'm old enough to go in there and not get in trouble."

Devlin laughed and slapped the boy on the back. "Boy, I ain't even old enough to go in there and not get in trouble!" She continued to laugh. "Stay here."

When Devlin walked into the front parlor, she knew her task wouldn't be easy. She casually fought off the advances of two young girls and went in search of the brothel's owner. Finally, she found Ellen handling a scuffle that had broken out between two of the working girls.

"Where's Sarah?" she asked.

"Come on, Stretch, she's in the back."

Ellen pulled the curtain aside for her, and all Devlin could see was Sarah moving backward toward Devlin, an amorous young man advancing on her.

"Look, I really don't work here," Sarah said as she continued to back up toward the door.

The young man saw the newcomers before Sarah did, but she realized it herself when she backed into a wall of warm body. Sarah knew in an instant that it was Devlin, the comforting scent of leather and wood-smoke assailing her nostrils.

Devlin felt Sarah's body press against her chest, and all rational thought left her. Devlin looked at the man, her blue gaze turning as pale as two chips of ice. He didn't seem to get the message, moving another step closer to Sarah. Devlin's involuntary response was a low growl that started deep in her chest.

Sarah felt the vibration against her back. She had heard the sound before. When she was a little girl, she had placed her hand too close to one of the family dogs while it enjoyed a bone. The threatening growl that came from the woman behind her sounded just like that dog's snarl. Sarah knew in her heart that the sound meant the same thing now as it did then: Back off because I don't understand the concept of sharing.

The young man was evidently a lot less stubborn than Sarah had been. Whereas she had teased the dog until she eventually was bitten, the man threw up his hands and took two steps back.

"She ain't worth fightin' over, friend," he drawled.

That's where you're wrong, Devlin thought.

Ellen took the young man by the arm and led him from the room, introducing him to a more willing companion.

"Are you all right?" Devlin asked.

"I'm fine, thank you…again. You're timing is impeccable." Sarah smiled brightly and Devlin felt her knees go a little weak.

The two sat at the table, waiting for Ellen to reappear. Sarah poured Devlin a drink and Devlin's blue eyes sparkled as the liquid slid down her throat. Grabbing the bottle, she looked at the label, then back at Sarah, one eyebrow nearly vanishing under ebony bangs.

"Well, I have to get it from somewhere," Sarah said, followed by a wry smile.

Devlin couldn't hold her curiosity back any longer. "How in the world do you know Ellen?"

"She's just an old friend."

"Don't let that pretty face fool ya, Stretch." Ellen walked into the room again. "This one's as shrewd a business woman as they come. Five years ago, when I didn't have a dime left to keep this place going, do ya think those nice, respectable cattlemen would help me out? They used the place plenty but didn't want their wives to know it." Ellen sat and poured herself another drink. She watched Devlin, who in turn, gazed at Sarah. Sarah stared into her glass.

"Frankly, it scared the hell out of me. This little slip of a girl waltzes into my place in broad daylight and plunks five hundred dollars in my lap. At first, I thought she wanted to bed me, and I just knew I was going to have to pull all the tricks out of the bag to earn that kind of money!" Ellen laughed aloud.

Devlin discovered Sarah's face was turning a nice shade of pink.

Sarah remembered the incident, too. She mostly remembered how badly her knees had shaken when she walked in and asked to speak to the owner. Then when she had begun to comprehend what the older woman thought she was going to have to do for the money, Sarah had nearly fainted dead away.

She never told Peter, but Sarah expected he had heard it from some of the men. If he had, he never brought it up. It was her money, and Peter always knew that Sarah moved to the beat of an unconventional drummer. Sarah had been determined to find herself damned before allowing the cattlemen to run Ellen out of town. So she withdrew the money and handed it over to the stranger.

"She just gives me the money and says she don't care what kind of business I'm in, but she'll die before she gives in to Montgomery and his cronies. She told me I could pay it back when I could, if I wanted. Only trouble was, I never wanted to. Kind of liked havin' this headstrong gal as my business partner." Ellen smiled and reached over to place a hand on top of Sarah's, receiving a sweet smile from her friend.

"And deep down, I don't think Sarah wants me to, either. I think she kinda likes spittin' in those fellas' eyes this way. A respectable lady like her ownin' a whorehouse."

Devlin hadn't said a word throughout the story. On the surface, she seemed to be handling things rather well, but underneath, the news had rocked her world. *It's not bad news, definitely not a bad thing. God, the last thing I ever wanted was a pristine virgin. This one may be a lady, but she's got quite a set of jewels on her.* Devlin found that she liked that. She liked that a lot.

Sarah and Devlin eventually said their goodbyes to Ellen and made their way outside. As Hannah leapt into her mother's arms, Ellen discreetly pulled Devlin aside. "You take good care of her, Stretch. You'll never find anyone who could love you more."

After securing the supplies and making everyone comfortable, Devlin led the wagon homeward. She liked the sound of that…home.

After an hour of silence, Sarah whispered to Devlin. "Me…silent partner in a brothel. Is that the one you never saw coming?"

"Completely blindsided me," Devlin said without missing a beat.

Another few moments of silence ticked by before Sarah spoke again. "Does it bother you?"

Devlin smiled at the worried frown on Sarah's face. Reaching over, she placed a warm hand on the smaller one of her friend. "Not one little bit." Devlin's smile grew larger. "It's the kind of thing…" She lowered her voice to barely a whisper, "…I guess it's the kind of thing only you would do for somebody. It makes me glad I'm…"

She wanted to say the words. *It makes me glad that I'm in love with a woman like you.* She couldn't muster the courage.

"…It makes me glad I'm your friend," Devlin finally finished.

By the look in Devlin's eyes, Sarah felt sure that Devlin had wanted to say more, but Devlin turned her gaze back toward the road, her smile returning when she felt Sarah's arm slip through her own.

"Oh, I almost forgot. Do you think you can make it look like ten blankets were a gift from the spirits to that young couple we met today?" Sarah asked.

"I'm sure I can," Devlin said with a smile.

Chapter Eight

"I don't like this idea, Sarah, not one bit." Devlin flashed electric blue eyes at Sarah.

Sarah was dressed in her customary riding outfit, which meant her son's clothes. Devlin had saddled Telemachus but had also been arguing for the last half hour with the stubborn blonde about taking the stallion out.

"It's not like I haven't done this before. It's only twenty-five miles to Uncle Art's place. I'll spend the day with the kids and Mattie and be home before the sun sets."

Matthew and Hannah were spending a few weeks at her uncle's ranch, playing and visiting with their cousins. Mattie offered to come out to the Double Deuce, but Sarah missed her children desperately after a few days. The ride over to her uncle's ranch was a pleasant one and Sarah didn't mind spending the time alone, even though she thought it would have been even nicer to have the beautiful wrangler along for company.

"I'll come with you," Dev said, nearing the end of her patience.

Sarah stopped and folded her arms across her chest. "And just who would be running herd over this fine ranch of ours while you're babysitting me?"

Devlin searched her brain, only to find herself unable to formulate a response. She opened her mouth a couple of times but couldn't keep her tongue from getting in the way.

Devlin groaned loudly. Turning and stomping back into the

house, she came out with one of the Winchester rifles from over the mantel.

"All right, don't shoot, I won't go," Sarah teased with her hands in the air.

Devlin glared at Sarah and her untimely sense of humor. Devlin double-checked the rifle and slid it into its leather holster on the left side of the saddle, stuffing an extra box of cartridges into the saddlebag. She pulled one of her own six guns from its holster and made sure it was loaded. Devlin then held the pistol out for Sarah.

"Dev—"

"Look, you should be honored at how much I trust you. I've never, ever let anyone use one of my guns before."

"But, Dev—"

"It's just a little added protection. Keep it in your belt while you're riding, like this—"

"Dev," Sarah said once more in a loud voice, her small hand stopping to wrap around Devlin's slender one. "I don't know how to shoot one of these."

"What?"

"I said—"

"I heard you the first time, I just can't believe it! You mean to tell me you can shoot the wings off a gnat at fifty yards with a rifle, but you've never fired a pistol before?"

Sarah gave a lopsided grin and shrugged her shoulders.

"Okay," Dev said, half dragging Sarah out onto the open prairie and away from the house. "All you have to do is raise it, pull back the hammer, and shoot." She demonstrated by raising the gun, cocking the hammer with her thumb, and shooting a small branch off a nearby tree. Then she handed the pistol to Sarah.

Sarah did exactly as Devlin had instructed. Devlin happily watched Sarah's strong hand easily pull back the hammer. Sarah fired the gun and an old tin can flew from a nearby post. She beamed up at Devlin.

"Not bad, huh?"

"Sarah," Devlin drawled. "Did you mean to hit that can?"

"Um...no, actually, I was shooting at the same tree you hit." Sarah grinned sheepishly, indicating the tree ten feet left of the post.

Devlin shook her head and ran her hand across her face. Grasping the gun from Sarah's hand, she reloaded it and stuck it in Sarah's belt. Then the two walked back to where Devlin had saddled Telemachus.

"Let's just hope that anyone that means to give you trouble will take one look at it and think you know how to use it," Devlin said.

Sarah buttoned her jacket, turning toward Devlin. "If you expect me to kill anyone with this, he's going to have to start trouble about ten feet to my left," Sarah joked.

A look of pain passed across of Devlin's face. "Sarah..." She reached over and pulled open Sarah's jacket and slipped the gun from Sarah's waist. "I don't want you to have to kill anyone...ever."

"Why?" Sarah asked in confusion. "I mean, I'm not real anxious to, either, but why the change of heart?"

"Because taking another person's life changes things. It changes everything," Devlin said, her eyes unable to meet Sarah's.

Sarah tenderly squeezed Devlin's forearm. "It's all right, Dev. I'll be fine, you'll see."

Devlin wanted to put her arms around Sarah and kiss her for all she was worth, but she just stood there as Sarah turned to mount the black horse. After Devlin gave her a foot up, Sarah reached her hand down to grasp Devlin's.

"I'm not used to anyone riding herd over me. Guess I'm not used to someone worrying about me for a change."

"Get used to it," Dev couldn't help saying.

"Don't forget to eat something," Sarah called back before she was out of sight.

Massive black thunderheads gathered over the north ridge.

The sun had long before hidden behind the approaching storm clouds, and lightning flashes lit up the sky in the distance. Devlin paced back and forth outside the door to the cabin.

"Before the sun sets, she said. Before the sun sets. She promised me! Did she leave her uncle's or is she still there? Damn it, Sarah!"

Devlin continued to argue with herself. She didn't want Sarah to think she was treating her as some helpless child, but she was getting worried. The temperature had dropped considerably, and Devlin guessed that it had already started snowing in the mountains. A chill that caused her usually warm body to shiver made up her mind.

"To hell with your feelings about independence this time!"

Devlin hastily threw a few supplies in her saddlebag and looped a lantern's handle around the saddle horn. She shrugged on her heavy leather coat and took off, hopeful that she would meet up with the prodigal ranch owner.

"Easy, boy," Sarah said in gentle tones to the skittish stallion.

Another flash of lightning, closer than the last, jerked Sarah around in the saddle. Sarah used all the upper body strength she had to keep the reins pulled tight and down from the horse's head. The well-trained stallion did its best to follow Sarah's commands, but the flashes of light soon became accompanied by ear-splitting cracks of thunder. Telemachus reared once and Sarah fought him back down, jerking the bit roughly in a downward motion, struggling to keep her seat. The reins bit into Sarah's frozen fingers as she cursed herself for forgetting her riding gloves.

Sarah fought the large horse for control and was still winning the battle when a flare of lightning struck a tree to the right of the precariously rocky path they were on. Once again, Telemachus reared his front legs, Sarah snapping the reins around his neck sharply in a downward motion. When the horse's front hooves came down, they landed on the edge of the path. Without the solid ground under his hooves, the stallion panicked and his front feet started to slide down the wall of crushed rock over the edge of the path. Sarah desperately tried to maneuver the horse's head straight down the hill, but the panic-stricken animal kept trying to turn its body back uphill, until the loosened gravel swept his feet out from under him.

The right stirrup had trapped Sarah's foot, ensnaring her leg between the horse and the loose shards of rock. She couldn't tell if the screams she heard belonged to her or the horse as the crushed gravel carried them down the hill. The razor sharp shale bit and tore at the flesh of horse and rider. They finally skidded to a stop, chunks of dirt and rock still falling after them, beating into the unconscious woman's body.

It was some time later when Sarah awoke. She couldn't remember what pulled her awake first, the freezing cold, the rain pouring down in buckets, or the agonizing screams of the stallion that still lay on top of her right leg. The light was gone as darkness had enveloped them. The only source of illumination became the brilliant streaks of lightning exploding across the sky in large, jagged lines. With every flash of light, the horse jerked itself upward, screaming in pain. The horse's panicked movements not only pulled painfully on Sarah's leg, but also caused them to slide farther down the hill of loose rock.

Another flash of light and Sarah nearly screamed at the cause of the horse's agony. His front legs were broken badly, the limbs bent at odd angles, the hoof on one foot torn away completely. The animal jerked and twitched in pain as Sarah sobbed useless words of comfort to her longtime companion.

Blowing on her frozen fingers to bend them, she slid her Winchester from its leather holster. With a pain in her heart unlike any she'd ever had to bear, she leveled the barrel of the gun at the horse's head.

Straining her eyes in the darkness, the wind and rain beat unmercifully against Devlin's face. She had unrolled the long duster she kept behind her saddle as soon as the rain had begun to come down, but even that and the leather jacket she wore underneath couldn't keep out the sting of cold that seeped through.

A sound like thunder caught Devlin's attention. It sounded sharper, more like the crack of a rifle than a clap of thunder. Devlin spurred Alto toward the distant sound.

Reaching a fallen tree that had obviously been struck by lightning, Devlin knew Sarah could not have passed by the huge timber that blocked the path. She stopped and retraced her trail a half-dozen times but kept returning to the fallen tree. Dismounting, she walked along the edge of the path, searching for any signs of Sarah. She stopped at a spot on the edge of the rocky path where it looked as though gravel had been thrown about.

Grabbing the lantern from her saddle, she pushed her body back into a niche in the rock to light the kerosene lantern. Peering over the edge of the hill of crushed rock, Devlin couldn't be sure, but she thought she could make out a dark shadow.

"Sarah!" Devlin screamed out.

"Dev?" She heard the weak reply.

Tossing her rope over an outcropping of rock, Devlin looped it around her waist and made her way down the unstable hill of gravel. Devlin started out about six feet to one side of where she thought Sarah was, so she wouldn't pelt the woman with loose gravel on her way down.

"Sarah." Dev's voice cracked with emotion, but she didn't care.

She scrambled beside the fallen woman, but not before her weight shifted into the horse, causing Sarah to slide down the hill a few more feet.

"D-Dev," Sarah said in a hoarse voice. "D-don't hang on to me! I-I had to shoot T-Telem-machus. M-my foot is c-caught in the stirrup. He'll d-drag you d-down."

Sarah was freezing and couldn't stop shivering enough to

keep her teeth from chattering.

Devlin pulled the Winchester free of its holster and placed it on the rock next to Sarah. Next, she pulled the large bladed knife free from her boot. She eased her hand between the dead horse and Sarah's leg, stopping whenever she felt a shift in the horse's weight. After long moments, she could feel Sarah's booted foot, the stirrup snugly pressed against her heel. The rain stung as it blew into her eyes while she carefully sliced through the leather that held Sarah's leg prisoner.

"It's going to hurt when I pull," Devlin warned.

"I-it's okay. I-I'm too c-cold t-to feel it."

Devlin held on to Sarah with one arm around her waist and another around her shoulder. Placing one boot on the stallion's rump, Devlin gently pushed. It didn't take much for the sliding rock to carry the horse down the hill and off Sarah's leg. Dev didn't wait another minute. She wrapped her arms around Sarah and held her body to her own.

"Damn it, Sarah, you scared the hell out of me. Couldn't you have listened to me just once?" a frightened Devlin cursed.

"Hey, I-I'm h-having a b-bad day h-here, t-too. Poor T-Telem-machus." Sarah looked down the hill into the darkness in tears.

"I know, I know. I'm sorry," Devlin said sadly into Sarah's ear, holding her tighter. "You're freezing to death. Hold on to me. We've got to get you someplace where I can light a fire."

Devlin held on to Sarah with strong arms, pulling the two of them up the wall of rock. The rain still fell, but the wind had eased up. Finally reaching the ledge, Devlin was able to examine Sarah's leg under the light of the lantern. It was a good thing Sarah had worn her leather riding boots. They had withstood the worst of the damage. Above the boot, however, at mid-calf, the gravel had torn Sarah's pants away. The tattered flesh was raw and bleeding, bits of dirt and gravel embedded into the cuts. The only reason Sarah wasn't in complete agony was that she couldn't feel anything yet due to the cold.

Sarah could hardly move a muscle. She was sore, scared,

and frozen. Devlin easily lifted Sarah into her arms and mounted Alto. Unable to get past the fallen tree without going the long way around, Devlin debated whether Sarah was up for that. Devlin tucked Sarah on the saddle in front of her, Devlin's long duster wrapped around both of them.

Devlin tried to think quickly, realizing that it was hours back to the cabin. She headed up and from the path, pulling to a stop in front of a dense patch of cedar trees. The tops of the trees intertwined perfectly so that the ground underneath was soft and dry.

Once Devlin dismounted, she sat Sarah on the ground, her back against the trunk of the tree. Stripping Alto of saddlebags and saddle, Devlin tied the mare under a stand of trees where she, too, could stay somewhat dry. Devlin couldn't get the tinder to catch the wet wood, so she poured some of the kerosene on the logs and they had a roaring blaze in no time. The kerosene made the fire smoke a bit, but Devlin didn't think there would be anyone crazy enough to be out on such a night. She had to decide whether to work on Sarah's leg first or get the woman out of her soaking clothes. She opted for Sarah's injured leg, knowing the extreme pain involved in cleaning such a wound. Devlin wanted to get it over with before feeling began to seep back in.

"Sarah, I need to clean your leg up. It's going to hurt like nothing you've ever felt before, but it has to be done. If we let it linger even one day, you could end up losing it."

Sarah's eyes look like a frightened rabbit's, but she nodded.

Devlin laid her bedroll on the ground close to the fire. It was slightly damp, but she wanted to save the dry inner blanket to wrap around Sarah once she removed the wet clothes. Devlin turned Sarah's ankle, poking and prodding until she was satisfied that the ankle wasn't broken, then she removed Sarah's boots. Next came what was left of Sarah's torn and shredded pants. Devlin helped Sarah remove her soaked jacket and wrapped Devlin's dry one around Sarah. Devlin removed her own shirt and the white cotton shirt she wore underneath it. Looking up at Sarah, Devlin caught the woman staring at her body, and she nervously put her outer shirt back on.

"See, isn't it a good thing you make me wear a clean shirt every day?"

Devlin tore the white cotton undergarment into thin strips. Poised over Sarah's right leg, Devlin positioned Sarah on to her left side.

Devlin readied her canteen of water. "Ready?"

Sarah nodded and prepared for the worst. It didn't seem too bad at first until the combination of warm fire and water brought back a little sensation to her previously unfeeling skin. The agony started when Devlin gently scrubbed the dirt and embedded gravel from the wounds. Sarah cried out, then started crying in earnest. About halfway through, Devlin paused to let Sarah catch her breath.

Tears filled Devlin's eyes at Sarah's pain. Offering Sarah a drink of water, Devlin stroked her wet hair and brushed it from her face. They stayed that way until Devlin judged that Sarah's breathing wasn't quite as ragged.

"Just a little bit more, honey," Devlin whispered against Sarah's skin.

Sarah nodded, the term of endearment lost on her. Once again, Devlin began the laborious task of tending the wound. Closing her ears to Sarah's cries of pain, Devlin knew that if she stopped now, she wouldn't have the heart to begin again.

By the time Devlin finished, wrapping makeshift strips of bandage around Sarah's leg, Sarah's tears had turned to murmured sobs. Devlin was proud of Sarah, uncertain if she would have held up any better.

Devlin didn't ask first; she removed the rest of Sarah's clothing, draping them over some low hanging branches by the fire. If the circumstances hadn't been so extreme and Devlin hadn't been terrified over what would happen to Sarah, she might have had time to enjoy the exquisite body she carefully wrapped in a dry blanket. As it was, she could only think of the task at hand. Throwing a couple of additional limbs on the already blazing fire, Devlin lay beside the shivering woman. She rubbed Sarah's skin through the blanket to generate heat into Sarah's freezing frame.

Sarah's teeth chattered so loudly that Devlin didn't think Sarah would ever be able to relax. Devlin rose and kicked a few stones from the fire where she had initially set them. Moving them with the toe of her boot, she placed the warm rocks under the edge of the bedroll that Sarah lay upon, then lay down again on the other side of Sarah's shivering body.

Devlin reached under the blanket and rubbed her warm hands over Sarah's arms and back.

"How c-can you b-be so warm?" Sarah asked, amazed at Devlin's fortitude.

"I'm just that way." Devlin smiled to cover up her fear. "Does this bother you…being so, um, close?"

"I-I don't w-want you t-to take this the wrong w-way, D-Dev, but right now I-I'd lay d-down with John M-Montgomery to g-get warm!"

Devlin laughed and pulled Sarah closer so she was lying more on Devlin's body than the blanket. Devlin was thankful that Sarah still had her sense of humor along with her stubborn streak. Devlin had a feeling that Sarah would need them both.

To Devlin, it felt as though forever had passed, but her pocket watch showed that only a half hour had gone by since they lay under the blankets. Sarah still shivered uncontrollably and something about desperate times rang through Devlin's head. She unbuttoned her shirt, pulling it from her shoulders, and pressed Sarah's chilled skin against her own warm flesh, which grew more heated by the minute.

The feel of Sarah's breasts pressing into her own did dangerous things to Devlin's brain. Thankfully, however, she felt Sarah's skin respond and begin to warm. Continuing to caress Sarah's skin, Devlin finally heard only silence as the chattering of Sarah's teeth subsided. It must have been her imagination, but Devlin thought she felt Sarah's breath quicken at her delicate touch. In time, Sarah snuggled against Devlin's neck. They fell asleep with Sarah's deep, even breaths tickling Devlin's throat.

Devlin woke in the middle of the night to a parched throat and sweat dripping from her body. Her skin burned, but she quickly realized that it wasn't her body. She rolled Sarah off her and onto her back.

"Sarah," Devlin called out.

Sarah struggled to open her eyes, but she appeared to be unable to focus. Her eyes closed again and she mumbled a few words. Devlin couldn't grasp what she had said.

"Sarah, wake up. Come on." She stroked the unresponsive woman's cheek, which burned with its own fire.

Even though Sarah's body burned with fever, she shivered uncontrollably. Devlin jumped up and pulled her clothes on, replacing Sarah's now dry clothes. It took only minutes for her to douse their fire, pack their blankets, and saddle Alto.

"This isn't good, Sarah. This isn't good at all," Devlin said as she spurred Alto farther up into the mountains, Sarah tucked safely in front of her.

Devlin feared for the unconscious woman, knowing her own healing skills wouldn't be enough. It was too far for Sarah to travel back to town. By the time they reached a doctor, Sarah would be lucky to be alive.

There was only one place and to one group of people Devlin trusted enough to bring Sarah. She urged Alto on into the hills of the Thunderbird clan.

Chapter Nine

Dev knew that they watched her even as she navigated Alto through the hazardous rock formations overlooking the prairie. The mare wasn't used to the extra burden, but she bore the additional weight without complaint, picking her way among the sandstone boulders. The cedar trees were numerous and ancient this high up, and their trunks looked as gnarled and bent as old men.

The eyes that watched were curious but silent, following the two women all the way into the camp. The guards would have forced anyone else to stop before allowing them to reach the encampment of the Thunderbird clan, but the night watchers knew Redhawk. The woman was as fierce a warrior as any brave among them and had earned the respect they showed her. She was also the granddaughter of their *Miko*.

The sun was a short way from rising over the eastern hills as Devlin entered the camp. The rain and wind had long since ceased, but the cold rush of air told her winter would soon be here. She dismounted, taking care not to jostle the woman in her arms. She bent to one knee, rubbing a handful of the red earth on the top of each of Sarah's hands, then doing the same to her own hands. This was a sign of respect when entering the camp, to thank the spirits for providing the earth beneath their feet.

Devlin knew where she would go. Keeho was an excellent healer, but his visions frightened her. She had seen too many of them become truth to feel comfortable around the old man. If she needed a dream interpreted, she would seek out Keeho. What she needed now was someone who knew the ways of herbs and the human body, someone who could dream something pleasant. She headed straight for Tima's *chuka*. It didn't matter that Tima had painted new totems on the outside wall. Devlin knew that Tima was a widow now, and without a brave to provide for her, she would have had to go back to her father's fire. Being the widow of two brothers earned Tima the right to her own lodging, but it would always be set to the right of her father, *Miko* Kontonalah.

Devlin knelt on the ground at the entrance to the lodging.

"Tima, *Nali*...Tima..." The owner of a *chuka* was never under any obligation to answer to anyone outside her lodging in the middle of the night, but Devlin hoped the term of endearment she used to call her clan mother, *Nali,* or smiling one, would prompt the woman to answer.

The woman who came to the entrance and pulled the deer hide flap aside was perhaps fifteen years older than Devlin. Lines etched her brown skin around her mouth and at the corners of her eyes, but they were a testament to the fact that she smiled every chance she could. Fine gray threads swept through her long black hair and she held a blanket tucked closely around her shoulders. She smiled when she saw Devlin's face, but it quickly turned into a frown when she saw what her daughter held in her arms. Motioning Devlin into her home, Devlin carried Sarah in and laid her on the *topa*, the soft buffalo robe her mother gestured to.

The story spilled out of Devlin's mouth, half in English, half in the language of the clan. Her eyes filled with tears as she told of Sarah's injury. She sat back as her mother cupped a loving hand under her cheek and whispered soft words of comfort. It was so easy for Devlin to be open around Tima; in that respect, the older woman was like Sarah. The two most important women in Devlin's life had the same honest and loving natures.

Tima knew before her daughter had stepped foot into the

camp that Devlin would arrive soon. The older woman had a dream, and her dreams always became reality. Pulling the blanket off Sarah, Tima pushed Sarah's clothing into a pile. Her hands felt the death hanging over the white woman.

"This will have to be where we start. Come here and kneel," Tima commanded.

Devlin quickly complied, trying to stare anywhere but at Sarah's naked body lying on display before her.

Tima ran her hands through Devlin's hair and down her arms. "Have you killed recently?" There was no time for subtleties.

"It's been a long while."

The answer seemed to surprise the older woman. "You both have the feel of it on you."

Devlin's mind raced backward until it struck her. "Telemachus...her horse. Sarah had to put her horse down, his legs were broken."

Tima resumed her caresses of the girl's body. "Yes," she muttered. "Burn this...all of it." Tima pushed the pile of Sarah's clothes and the blanket toward Devlin. "Your clothes, too...boots, all of it. We must remove this *chukash* before he pulls your Little Salmon away, too.

Devlin would have told just about anyone else that they were insane and she wasn't about to burn a twenty-dollar pair of boots, but this was Tima. All living creatures had a *chukash*, it was their center, where their heart and spirit dwelled.

Tima explained that she felt the black stallion's *chukash* trying to take Sarah's life to wherever Telemachus had passed over. Tima had a healing gift, much like that of a medicine woman, and when there was concern in her voice, Devlin felt there was definitely something about which to worry. Without question, Devlin stripped off every stitch of clothing she wore, including her hat and boots. She was thankful that she had tucked her guns safely in her saddlebag.

Tima went into a dark recess of the *chuka* and brought out a large basket. Pulling the lid off, she reached in and unfolded a deerskin blanket, symbols of power and strength painted along the outer edges. She put it aside; she would need to cleanse Sarah first. Digging deeper, Tima brought out a buckskin outfit and handed it to her daughter. Devlin looked at the clothes in her hand and recognized them right down to the knee-high moccasin boots. Her adopted father, Tekola, had been a tall man. His clothes would fit her easily.

Tima gave careful instructions on how Devlin was to cleanse her body, first burning the clothes by the lake. Devlin turned to go, not caring that she was leaving the confines of the lodging naked. Most of these people had seen her naked at one time or another. Now she looked back at Sarah, pain in her eyes, until Tima nearly pushed her from the tent.

Once they were alone, Tima spoke to Sarah. "You must live, Little Salmon. I would very much like to hear your tale of Redhawk." Tima spoke to the unresponsive woman as she mixed herbs into a large bowl. "How did such a little fish catch such a fierce bird of prey?"

Devlin burned it all, everything that Sarah came in contact with, including Devlin's custom saddle. She wouldn't take any chances when it came to Sarah's well-being. Using the herbs Tima had given her, Devlin washed her hair and body in the freezing lake water, then dressed in the leathers her mother had presented to her.

"Aw, hellfire! I can't believe I forgot about this!"

The soft leather outfit was typical male dress. Devlin slipped her legs into the pants, which were more like leggings that tied at the hips. There was nothing to cover the crotch, or backside. A beaded loincloth covered those private parts. She pulled the decorative leather shirt over her head. It only came to her hips, and the cold, early morning air hit parts of her body that were used to being covered. The look didn't bother her at all. She looked like every other clan warrior over the age of maturity.

Returning to Tima's *chuka*, Devlin paused at the entrance

of the lodging. "*Tiana*?" She asked permission to enter.

"Come," Tima commanded.

Tima sat next to Sarah, trying to coax the woman to drink one of her teas, but having little success. She looked up at her daughter and smiled broadly at the familiar sight of her beloved mate's leathers.

"She will take it from you," Tima said, holding out the wooden bowl.

"How do you know?" Dev asked, slipping an arm around Sarah's shoulder to raise her head.

"A mother always knows her daughter's heart. I just know," Tima said cryptically.

Sarah opened her eyes and was sure she was dreaming. Devlin knelt by her side, dressed like an Indian brave. Sarah wanted to reach out and touch Devlin's face, but she couldn't make the muscles in her arms work. It almost felt as if she was floating.

"You are so beautiful," Sarah whispered instead.

Devlin's eyes sparkled and she could feel the hot flush rise to her face. "Thank you." She grinned.

"Dev, I'm so hot," Sarah complained, trying to push the leather covering off her fevered body.

Devlin grabbed Sarah's hands. "Sarah, I need you to drink some of this. It will help you get well." Devlin raised the bowl to the sick woman's lips.

Sarah took a small sip and swallowed the sweet liquid. "Where are we?" Sarah asked weakly.

"We're in the village of the Thunderbird clan. You kept asking me to bring you here, remember?" Dev encouraged Sarah to drink again.

Sarah turned her head toward Tima, who offered Sarah a smile filled with the light of the sun. Turning a questioning face back to Devlin, Sarah struggled to keep her eyes open.

"That's Tima," Devlin introduced her mother.

"I like her smile," Sarah whispered after taking another sip of the tea.

Devlin pulled Sarah closer to her and gently kissed her forehead. "If you call her *Nali*, she'll smile even more for you."

Sarah had fallen asleep again. Devlin tried to wake her, but Tima stilled her hand. "She needs to rest before the next step."

She had no idea what the next step was to be, but Devlin swore to herself that she would do anything it took to have her Sarah back.

As morning approached, Sarah's fever burned even hotter than the night before, and she developed a cough that wracked her body. None of Tima's medicines could stop the fever and chills that plagued Sarah, and when the terrible coughing began, Sarah's weak body ran out of strength. The muscles in her torso ached from the constant hacking cough until she could scarcely expand her chest to take a breath.

Devlin held Sarah in her arms, helping her to sit up when she would wake and the coughing fits overtook her, but soon Sarah fell deeper into the clutches of the fever and became unresponsive. Before long, her respirations came in small gasps as her lungs struggled to take in air.

All Devlin could do was to helplessly hold Sarah in her arms. A woman of action, Devlin felt more impotent with each passing moment. She could only watch as Sarah's life slowly slipped away.

"Do you see her *chukash*?" Dev asked her mother.

Tima sat close by, mixing together a new combination of herbs to try. She looked up from her work and stared at Sarah wrapped in her daughter's arms.

"Yes. It is thin, but her will is strong, but sometimes one's will alone cannot hold on to *chukash*." Tima watched her daughter caress Sarah's face and run her fingers through hair the color of sunlight.

"Does she know?" Tima asked.

Devlin raised a confused face to her mother.

"That you are in love with her," the older woman

continued.

"No," Devlin whispered, returning to gaze down at the flushed face of the woman who held her heart.

"Will you tell her?"

Devlin ran her fingertips against the warm, smooth edge of Sarah's cheek before answering. "No…I-I can't lose this… what we already have. I-I can't take that chance." She forced the sobs that threatened to break loose back down her throat.

"That does not sound like you, *Tasa*, unwilling to take a risk," Tima said softly.

Devlin smiled sadly at her mother, enjoying the way Tima's pet name for her rolled off the older woman's tongue. "It's different outside the clan. Sarah is different. The white man doesn't…they don't accept it, women together," Dev said brokenly, all the love in her heart becoming visible within her facial features. "I'll just have to be happy with the way things are," she murmured.

Two more days passed, but still Sarah slipped further into the grip of the illness that held her. Tima's dreams had made the older woman irritable and somewhat sharp-tongued toward Devlin. More than irritable, Tima was frightened for her Little Salmon. The previous night as she slept, Tima had watched as Sarah's *chukash* finally gave up and left her body. All the while, Devlin stood with her back to Sarah, ignoring her pleas. Tima knew the dream would become truth unless her daughter would listen to her own heart.

Tima placed a poultice on Sarah's chest, covering it with a rabbit skin. Devlin's voice pulled Tima from her worries.

"It's been two days," Devlin nearly hissed.

Tima worked slowly and methodically, not giving in to the same panic Devlin seemed to have developed, but she finally lost her patience. "Go! Go outside," Tima said sharply, pushing Devlin from the lodge. "Your worry will kill the girl!"

Tima turned her back on her daughter, but not before she caught the wounded look in Devlin's eyes. She hadn't meant for her words to be so harsh, but the dream from the previous night weighed heavily on her. She understood its meaning, knowing that Sarah's last hope would be Devlin, but could her daughter overcome her pride? Would she?

Devlin slipped back into the lodging, watching as her mother sang and rocked Sarah in her arms. Devlin felt as if her heart was breaking.

"*Asilhha imahaksichi am, Nali.*" Devlin's contrite head bowed to her mother, asking for forgiveness.

Tima laid Sarah's body back onto the blankets, turning to open her arms for her daughter. Tima accepted Devlin's apology and held her as Devlin's heartbreak turned into tears for her beloved Sarah. For a long time, Devlin lay cradled in the arms of her mother. Finally, Tima broke the silence.

"She needs more help than I can give. I have spoken with your grandfather. It is time to send up smoke."

Devlin pulled away to look into her mother's face.

"It is all we have left."

Devlin's jaw tightened and the corded tendons in her neck twitched slightly. To send up smoke meant only one thing. The elders and healers would gather around the ailing individual's family as they sent up the sacred smoke, along with their prayers. The smoke would alert the great spirit that they needed its help. The only problem was that Sarah had no family here. The closest thing she had was Devlin.

Tima watched the war that raged inside her daughter. It was easily viewable on Devlin's face. It would be a test of her daughter's commitment to Sarah to see if Devlin would comply. Tima's own heart remembered the pain of the last time she made such a request of her daughter. Her mate, Tekola, lay on his deathbed. Tima begged Devlin to walk around the medicine wheel and send up the smoke with her, but the proud young woman said that she could not. Devlin had refused to kneel to man or spirits, even in exchange for her father's life.

Devlin stood and ran her hands through her hair. Her gaze nervously darted back and forth as she searched her brain for another way. Tima hadn't meant to tell her daughter of her vision, but she saw Devlin teetering on the brink of indecision. The older woman would have to force Devlin to examine her heart if they were to keep Little Salmon's *chukash* with them in the land of the living. Tima didn't know if it would help or hinder, but she chose to be honest.

"I had a dream last night. It was about your Little Salmon."

Devlin sat next to her mother again. "Why didn't you tell me?"

"I'm telling you now," Tima said matter-of-factly. She paused for a moment, Devlin's blue eyes burning with questions. Tima then told Devlin all she had dreamed, then sat back and watched as dark clouds of pain passed across Devlin's face. "Do you see the same meaning that I do in these dreams, *Tasa*?"

All Devlin could do was look at Sarah, lying helpless on the ground. She understood the meaning of her mother's dream easily enough. Devlin was the only one who could offer up smoke on Sarah's behalf, and it was the one thing she could never debase herself enough to do.

Silent minutes passed until Devlin stood and left the tent. "I can't," she whispered to her mother. "I just can't."

Devlin ran from the village. She ran until she had no breath left and found herself among the jagged rocks, listening to the sound of the water falling into the deep pool below. This was where she would come and hide as a child. Although she already killed a man by the time Tima and Tekola had adopted her, she was little more than a girl. Children's cruel remarks cut deeply, and many times Redhawk would climb up to the rocks to get away and find what little peace she could for her soul.

What Tima asked of her—no, what they expected of her—tore at Devlin's heart. She had admitted that she would do anything for Sarah. Now Devlin questioned her love, the depth of her commitment to Sarah. She questioned if she truly did love Sarah that much. Devlin looked to the sky, wondering how many times she would have to suffer through the death of someone she loved. She had waited a lifetime for a woman to walk into her life, a woman who was everything Sarah was.

Devlin remembered what it felt like living within the clan, the first time she had been able to look at a woman openly, the freedom she felt at not having to hide her feelings of appreciation for another woman's beauty. Whereas the white man had called her an abomination, these people thought the spirits had blessed her. Devlin happily realized that she wasn't the only member of the clan who had feelings for members of the same sex. The tribe looked at this as a gift, like being a healer or a medicine woman. It wasn't something the spirits touched everyone with, therefore the clan considered it something special bestowed upon human beings.

When Devlin grew older and left the clan, she used sex as a tool, a weapon of power over the men she commanded. It wasn't as if sex never held any physical enjoyment, but she could only achieve her release when she was in control. Sex had become a mere physical act, nothing more. The only emotion she ever allowed herself had been the thrilling feeling of a partner's surrender. It became a sort of victory, a conquest. Back then, Devlin had thought sentiments like love and devotion would only make her weak. Because of her ideas toward sex, there were always things she never let men do to her, and in turn, acts she never performed for them. She would never bow or give up control to anyone. Back then, sex had all the pleasure of a written negotiation.

Now there was Sarah. Devlin longed to love Sarah that way, to give herself up to the blonde's caring touch. She could scarcely hold the heartache in as she balled her hands into fists, throwing back her head and howling out her frustration to the sky. Devlin let the tears come, holding her head in her hands. The examination of her heart came at such a price. After so many years, Devlin finally understood the union between emotion and sex. It had taken a farm girl from Kentucky to

give Devlin back what she had waited so long to find again...
her soul.

"What good will smoke be with no prayer to follow?"
Keeho said to Tima, shaking his head sadly.

Miko Kontonalah and the other elders sat in a semicircle,
the ring closed at one end by Sarah's prone figure, the sound
of her wheezing filling the tent. Kontonalah would have liked
to speak to his granddaughter, but she was nowhere in sight. If
Redhawk did not want to be found, she would not be.

A cold draft of air swept through the lodging when a hand
swept the deer hide flap aside. The figure that entered caused a
number of silent nods and even a few low whispers, but Tima's
gray eyes misted at the sight.

Devlin knelt before her grandfather in respect, the old man
placing a gentle hand on her head. In turn, Devlin knelt before
each elder. When Devlin knelt before her mother, Tima could
barely form words. Her pride was so great. Devlin looked
anxiously at her mother, finally relaxing when the older woman
nodded her approval.

Devlin knelt before Keeho, the healer, last. He held out
two small clay jars of paint, one red and one black. Dipping his
index finger into one color and his middle finger in the other,
he let his coated fingertips glide against the skin of Devlin's
cheek, then he repeated the process on the other side.

Devlin stood before the small fire in the middle of the
circle as Keeho carefully fed a bundle of dried sage into the
flames. Once the smoke started to rise into thin tendrils around
Devlin's body, Devlin drew it to her in cupped hands, washing
it over her body in a ritual act of cleansing.

Devlin moved to stand over Sarah. She would visualize the
Thunderbird clan's interpretation of the medicine wheel in her
mind. Then Devlin would perform the most difficult act of her
life. Keeping her eyes on the face of the beautiful woman who
had saved her life and her soul, Devlin dropped to her knees.
Raising her hands over her head, the palms facing each other,

Devlin bent and bowed to the earth three times. The third time her body bent over, she continued to lie against the ground, while the chants of the elders began.

Tima watched her daughter through tear-filled eyes. The woman, who would humble herself to neither man nor God, prostrated herself in the ultimate act of submission for the life of her soul mate.

Even as the elders behind her continued to sing and chant, Devlin finished her prayers and made her way to Sarah. Sitting behind Sarah, Devlin tenderly pulled the unconscious form into her lap, wrapping her strong arms around the still figure. Devlin turned her face into Sarah's hair and breathed in the scent of sage. The dried herb continued to burn and permeated the air, its pleasant odor clinging to Sarah's skin. Devlin's lips brushed along the heated skin at Sarah's temple, and she gently rocked the woman in her embrace.

Devlin had finally come to that elusive place in her life, the one where her grandfather had told her all points converged. Some people never came to that segment in their lives; some passed it by, never recognizing it for what it was. As Devlin held the ill woman in her arms, she realized this was her time. Everything she ever knew, had ever felt became as nothing compared to what she experienced just then. Everyone and everything else in the tent disappeared into shadow. There was only Sarah, Devlin's love for Sarah, and the supplications of a dark warrior, whose prayers rose up on the wings of the sacred smoke.

Chapter Ten

Tima pulled the deerskin flap to one side and entered the *chuka*. The heavy smell of healing herbs still hung in the air, the sweet smell assaulting her nostrils. She had slept with relatives the previous night, leaving her daughter alone with her companion. Devlin still lay much the same as when Tima had left her, her arms wrapped protectively around the blond woman, whose back was pulled tightly against Devlin's chest. It appeared as if both women still slept soundly.

She went about her work but felt a sudden presence. When she turned, Tima noticed Sarah's eyes fluttering open and staring in confusion. Devlin's hand lay splayed across Sarah's abdomen and she unconsciously entwined her fingers into Devlin's hand. Leaning back against Devlin's chest, the tiniest bit of Sarah's mouth curled upward in a smile.

Tima smiled at Sarah's actions, thinking that her daughter should not have feared to tell Sarah of her feelings.

Sarah became conscious of Tima's gaze and cheerful smile. Quickly disentangling her fingers from Devlin's hand, she smiled back at the woman.

"Our prayers were answered quickly," Tima said, moving over to place a hand against Sarah's forehead. Sarah's face felt cool to her touch and Sarah breathed easy, no sign of the cough left.

Sarah struggled with her aching muscles to sit up. Her Choctaw wasn't perfect, and even though she spoke in halting, unsure tones, Tima understood her perfectly. Sarah surprised herself by understanding most of what the other woman told her about the past few days. Tima brought a waterskin and hot broth, both of which Sarah promptly made disappear. Devlin slept heavily the entire time.

"Tima, is there a place I can go to wash, to clean up? Between you and me, I feel like day-old trash," Sarah said shyly.

Tima nodded. Her heart soared at the recovery Sarah had made seemingly overnight. Understanding Sarah's need for modesty, Tima wrapped a soft robe of rabbit and fox skins around her and helped her to her feet. Sarah felt wobbly and unsure of her steps, but the older woman's strength surprised her, and Sarah leaned heavily on Tima.

Tima walked slowly, wrapping a strong arm around Sarah's waist. Sarah's leg was sore, but the cuts had begun to heal nicely. A young woman of perhaps fourteen or fifteen ran up to the pair. She grinned at Sarah, beginning to ramble on about what an honor it was to meet her.

"Little Dove," Tima scolded. "Let the poor girl get her feet under her first."

Little Dove looked heartbroken and Sarah couldn't help but smile at the young girl, uncertain why she would think of Sarah as something special.

"It's all right, Tima. It's very nice to meet you, Little Dove," Sarah said in a halting tongue.

Little Dove had wanted to meet the stranger for herself. She had a teenage crush on Redhawk for the past two seasons, always hoping the tall warrior would notice her when visiting the village. She heard from older girls that the small stranger was Redhawk's mate and that the beautiful warrior had prayed and cried in anguish at the thought of losing her beloved. When the girl saw the white woman's smile and easy demeanor, she knew in an instant why Redhawk had given her heart away. And as teenage hearts are fickle things, Little Dove switched allegiances and began to lose her heart to the blonde with the captivating green eyes.

Tima watched and knew Little Dove's crush to be misplaced, but she said nothing, then shook her head.

"Little Dove, you may do Little Salmon a service," Tima said.

The actual word was *favor*, but Sarah couldn't translate the word and had to settle for *service* in her understanding of the clan's language.

"Salmon needs something to wear. Perhaps you have something that would fit her," Tima said.

Little Dove's eyes lit up, and she rushed away to her family's *chuka*. Tima and Sarah shared quiet laughter at the girl's youth and enthusiasm.

"It's not like Dev...um, Redhawk to sleep so sound. Do you think she's all right?" Sarah asked once they had arrived at a secluded pool on the river. The weather had warmed considerably as if summer was only beginning and not ending.

"She has been awake for many days and nights watching over you, Little Salmon. It is good my daughter sleeps now."

"Dev is your daughter? I mean, Redhawk. I'm sorry, but I'm not used to calling her that."

"Yes." Tima smiled proudly. "Redhawk had just entered womanhood, still a young girl when she first came to the clan, but as beautiful as any maiden I had ever seen. My mate, Tekola, and I gladly raised her as our own. She was headstrong and stubborn, but she also proved to be brave and intensely loyal. One day, Redhawk confided to me that she preferred to take another woman as a mate instead of a brave, so Tekola taught her the ways of the warrior so she would be able to provide for a companion at her fire."

Tima went on to tell Sarah amusing stories about Redhawk's formative years. Sarah knew Devlin would be livid if she realized they were talking about her this way, but Sarah was fascinated with the dark-haired beauty she had fallen so in love with. Sarah felt as though she needed the connection to Devlin's past and hung on Tima's every word.

Tima helped Sarah wash her hair in the cool water of the river. Sarah was still trying to process everything that Tima had told her about Devlin.

"She just came right out and told you then...that she wanted to take a woman as a mate?" Sarah asked timidly.

Tima remembered what Redhawk had said about the white man's culture, that he did not accept two women as mates and even condemned those who the spirits had given such a gift. Tima wanted to be honest with Sarah, but she also wanted to learn if Sarah's heart truly held love for her daughter.

"Yes, it was only when she felt that I would not betray her trust. Redhawk told me of the way the white man feels about those with the gift. It must not be easy for you to live with all the white man's rules," Tima finished with a look of compassion.

"The gift?" Sarah asked.

Tima went on to explain the way the clan looked upon people who were different.

Sarah was astounded that these people took the idea of women together so easily. It gave her cause to hope. At least now Sarah had her confirmation that Devlin did indeed prefer women. Now all she had to do was to figure out a way to become that woman.

I can't even believe I'm thinking like that, but it's what I feel, isn't it?

"Did Dev, I mean, Redhawk...did she ever take a mate?" Sarah tried to sound nonchalant.

Tima was not to be fooled so easily, however. She heard the real question in Sarah's voice, saw the twinge of envy in the intelligent eyes. Tima would have to answer carefully.

"No, she never found the heart she would give up her wild ways for. She has always been like the *puma*. Wild and fierce, but I heard a story once, of a woman who was said to have tamed a *puma*. She was the only person the creature would appear tame around. Where she went, the animal followed. It is said that the woman's spirit so thoroughly captured the heart of the wild animal that when her *chukash* left this earth to fly with the spirits, the beast lay down and his heart stopped beating.

"That's such a beautiful story," Sarah said as Tima helped her comb and braid her honey-colored locks. "Do you think Redhawk could ever lose her heart like that?"

Tima smiled and turned Sarah so they faced each other. Gently grasping Sarah's chin, Tima looked with love at the woman who was quickly becoming like a daughter to her. "I think only you would know the answer to that question." Tima smiled knowingly.

Sarah looked away shyly from the woman's intense but loving gaze. A thousand questions flew through her mind. Did she own Devlin's heart that way? Had Devlin spoken to her mother about Sarah? *Oh, Dev, how can I find out without losing our friendship?*

Little Dove halted the questions in Sarah's mind when she rushed up to the pair of women as they sat on the ground. The girl handed Sarah a soft, fawn-colored buckskin dress and calf-length moccasins. The dyed trim and beadwork were more beautiful than anything Sarah had ever seen.

Oh, Little Dove, I couldn't possibly accept this. It's too beautiful." Sarah tried to hand the gift back. "I have nothing to give you in return, nothing as special as this."

Little Dove's eyes shone and she dropped to her knees. "It would be a good exchange if you would give me your friendship in return."

Sarah smiled brightly and placed her hand over the girl's. "You don't have to give me anything for me to be your friend."

Little Dove smiled crookedly but looked as though she was having difficulty breathing. Sarah felt the pulse in the girl's wrist quicken at her touch. Sarah had witnessed enough teenage boys react that way to recognize a crush when she saw one.

"Do you need help dressing?" Little Dove asked.

"No!" Sarah said more forcefully than she had intended. "Um, Tima will help me. Thank you, though."

"Go now, girl," Tima ordered, and Little Dove obediently ran off.

Sarah sighed deeply and looked over at Tima. Tima laughed aloud at Sarah's new dilemma. Even though Tima wasn't Devlin's birth mother, Sarah recognized how much the older woman reminded her of Devlin.

"I could be in trouble here, couldn't I?" Sarah asked with a weak smile.

"It's to be expected when one is so beautiful," Tima said, followed by more laughter.

Tima helped Sarah into the clan apparel. Once Sarah was dressed, she felt much more human. Her stomach growled, and she was still unsteady on her feet. When Tima helped Sarah to stand, a wave of dizziness hit her, and she grabbed the older woman's arms to keep from falling.

"Come, put your arm around me. Perhaps I let you do too much, too soon," Tima said with reproach.

It finally filtered through to Devlin's resting subconscious that the comforting feeling of a warm body next to her had disappeared. The sun had begun to seep into the *chuka* through the top opening when Devlin pulled herself awake. A fleeting moment of panic swept through her, quickly becoming fear. Jumping from the sleeping robes, Devlin rushed from the lodge, and stopped in her tracks.

Devlin's breath caught in her throat, a small gasp was the only sound she was able to make. Sarah walked along with Tima, Sarah's arm wrapped firmly around the older woman's waist. Tima had the girl pressed close to her, taking slow careful steps. Tima then said something to Sarah and Sarah laughed.

Seeing Sarah in clan garments was a shock to Devlin's libido. Even with dark circles under her eyes and a little weight gone, Sarah was the most beautiful woman Devlin had ever laid eyes on. Devlin fell in love all over again.

Devlin did something she rarely did. She acted without thinking. So moved by the vision of Sarah, healthy and alive,

Devlin practically ran to the woman and wrapped her arms around her.

"Good morning, sleepyhead," Sarah whispered into Devlin's ear, thoroughly enjoying the embrace.

Reluctantly, Devlin pulled away. Looking into Sarah's eyes, she reached up and stroked Sarah's cheek. Sarah smiled at the expression of concern looking down on her and moved her own hand to cradle Devlin's. Once again, Devlin couldn't resist and pulled Sarah into her arms, quickly leaning down to kiss the top of her head, then pulled back to look at her.

"How do you feel?" Devlin finally found her voice.

"Well, I'll probably drop like a sack of potatoes if you let me go, but all in all, I feel pretty good," Sarah said, squeezing Devlin's forearms.

"Then I won't let you go," Devlin said softly.

The look in Devlin's eyes nearly convinced Sarah that she owned the wild, untamed heart of this *puma*.

Devlin managed to tear her gaze away from the vision in front of her long enough to help Sarah back into the *chuka*. Noticing Sarah still had a slight limp from when the horse fell on her, Devlin gently helped Sarah to sit on the *topa* and then relaxed next to her. A few minutes later, Tima entered with some tea and a pot of stew that smelled wonderful to Sarah. There were no spoons, but Devlin showed Sarah how to scoop up the thick stew with rolled pieces of flatbread.

After eating their fill, both women thanked Tima, and she accepted their gratitude.

"So what were you two up to while I was sleeping?" Devlin asked suspiciously.

"Your mother helped me take a bath, and I met a girl named Little Dove who gave me the clothes I'm wearing," Sarah said.

Devlin raised an eyebrow in surprise. She knew Little Dove had one of those schoolgirl crushes on her, but she thought it best not to mention it to Sarah.

"I also learned that the people here consider modesty kind

of low on the priority list, I tried to go with it," she said to a smiling Devlin. "Everyone here keeps calling me a fish, which I'm very confused about, but I didn't even know how to ask them about it," Sarah finished in a whisper.

Devlin laughed aloud and promised to tell Sarah the story later.

"I also heard some rather amusing tales about a certain young warrior named Redhawk." Sarah smirked back at Devlin.

Devlin's face took on a gray cast as she attempted to glare at her mother. "Oh, you didn't."

"I think I like the one about you, the skunk, and the bow and arrow best," Sarah said, beginning to enjoy the way Devlin squirmed.

"*Nali*! You didn't!" Devlin said, thoroughly humiliated.

"You should have told me if you never wanted me to say anything," Tima said.

Devlin shook her head and rewarded Sarah with a lopsided grin. "Just wait till I get a chance to talk to your sister."

Sarah returned the laughter, suddenly growing serious. "Oh, Dev, how long have we been here, the children must be—"

Devlin silenced her with a raised hand. "It's okay. I sent a friend with a message down to Hank. He's been staying at the Double Deuce riding the herd. He sent a message back yesterday saying everything was fine, but he finished off the apple pie you baked before all this happened. I didn't want your uncle or the kids to worry. I didn't tell them about the injury or you being so sick. I hope I did the right thing."

"Yes, that was perfect. I'm so glad we have someone like Hank around."

"Okay, now you need rest," Tima said, pushing Sarah's still weak body to a reclining position.

"Yep, she's your mom, all right," Sarah teased. "I feel like I've already slept for a fortnight."

"Would you like me to stay here with you? I mean, just until you fall asleep?" Devlin asked, unwillingly to leave.

Sarah nodded, and as Tima left the lodging with a smile, Devlin lay on her side next to Sarah. She explained all that Sarah had missed over the last few days. Devlin also told her about the reason the clan called her Little Salmon, and when Sarah begged for more, Devlin told her stories of when she lived with the clan. Sarah could hardly contain her laughter when Devlin told her in detail about the skunk incident. Eventually realizing that she had spoken more in the past two hours than at any other time in her life, Devlin looked over at Sarah to discover she had fallen asleep.

Devlin had slept so long earlier that morning that she wasn't tired, but she rolled over onto her stomach and watched Sarah as she slept. She observed the gentle rise and fall of Sarah's chest and remembered when this—a woman such as Sarah for her life mate and a comfortable *chuka* to lodge in—was all she had ever wanted out of life. Finally, she had reached a point in her life where she thought the dream might be something more than a vision. She could only hope that Sarah would someday feel the same way.

Chapter Eleven

For the next two days, Tima allowed Sarah to rest and recuperate. By the third day of inactivity, Sarah put her foot down, and Tima knew that her patient was finally well.

Sarah enjoyed the people of the clan and their village. She met Tima's friends, watched as they worked and played, and learned many of their skills, all under the ever-present scrutiny of Little Dove. The girl showed up wherever Sarah was, waiting for some small bit of attention that Sarah might pay her.

On the third day in the village, Sarah had to lecture Devlin, in front of the other warriors of the clan, just to get her to leave Sarah's side for a few moments. She loved Devlin and her company, but Sarah wasn't accustomed to people hovering over her. It seemed to do the trick. Once a number of braves started laughing at the confused Devlin, she gave Sarah a bit more freedom.

Devlin didn't dare tell Sarah what an embarrassment it had been when Sarah took her down a notch in front of the braves who had stood watching. Devlin tried to slink away after the lecture she had received, but some of the young men were too amused to let it go.

Kaylan, Devlin's uncle, couldn't resist pouring salt in the wound. "Redhawk," the older man called out. "That bit in your mouth must feel awfully uncomfortable with the reins held so tight!"

Every man within hearing distance broke out into raucous laughter. Devlin growled under her breath and strode off in a different direction.

Later in the day, Sarah returned to Tima's *chuka* to find Devlin lying on the sleeping robes, her hands clasped behind her head. Devlin's brow furrowed as if she was deep in thought. She quickly sat up when she realized Sarah entered the tent.

"Hi," Sarah said brightly, taking a seat next to Devlin.

"Well, you're talking to me at least. That's a good sign," Devlin said, wearing an apologetic half-smile.

"I'm sorry about earlier. I started to feel like you didn't trust me to do anything on my own. I hope I didn't embarrass you too much."

The smile turned into a smirk. "Nah, it's okay. I deserved it. I guess I've been taking care of you and protecting you for so many days here…well, I guess I forgot you're not a thing to be protected."

"I haven't even thanked you for everything you did for me. I owe you."

Devlin reached out, and with the backs of her fingers, laid a feather-light caress across the line of Sarah's cheek. "For all that you've given me, you'll never owe me."

Feeling like she needed to change the subject, Devlin brought up the upcoming evening's festivities.

"Are you sure you feel up for tonight?" Devlin asked.

"I wouldn't miss it for the world. I'm terrified I'll do something to embarrass myself, though. Will you be…um, there…with anyone?" Sarah asked coyly. Tima had told her that the warm evening and the full moon made it a night for couples.

"I was thinking of taking a date." Devlin leaned back.

"Oh" was all Sarah said. She managed to remove the hurt from her voice but not the crestfallen look on her face.

Devlin continued to grin at Sarah, raising her eyebrows as if waiting for an answer.

"Oh." Realization dawned bright. "Me?"

"Who else?" Devlin laughed, enjoying the pink blush that

had settled on Sarah's cheeks. "Oh, don't ever change, Sarah. You're too perfect just the way you are." Devlin finished by touching the tip of her index finger to Sarah's nose, and they each shared some good-natured laughter.

A short time later, Sarah wandered away from the village. She had watched the women preparing some of their traditional dishes for that evening's dinner. Tima still would not allow Sarah to do anything too tiring, but she watched with interest how the clan women made small steamed biscuits out of cornmeal, wrapping them in corn husks to cook. The men and women alike were skilled farmers, making corn grow in the most unlikely places.

They cleared away small patches along the hillside to make room for the corn and bean crops. Aside from these crops, the clan made use of the world around them. They hunted for meat and collected nuts and berries when in season. Sarah had learned a great deal in the time she had been there.

Sitting at the top of a small hill, Sarah listened to the wind as it rustled the leaves of dried corn stalks. Sarah had discovered that in another fortnight, even the stalks would be cleared from this hillside patch. They wouldn't be plowed under as she had seen some of the white farmers do. The clan women and children would cut and save the stalks to burn during the winter months when firewood became scarce.

She watched the buffalo move across the prairie in large herds. This had been the first time since arriving in the village that she had a moment to herself. If Tima and Devlin weren't watching over her, Little Dove spied her out.

"So this is where you come to hide." Tima's voice seemed to come out of nowhere. She sat beside Sarah.

"Well, no, not hiding...exactly."

Tima looked at Sarah with a knowing expression that Sarah had come to know rather well.

"Oh, okay, but I just wanted a little time to myself."

"Should I go? I do not wish to disturb you."

"No, stay please. I like your company."

"Thank you. You have become like a member of the clan to me."

"You flatter me."

Sarah looked off into the distance once more, but her gaze wasn't focused on the buffalo. Tima saw many emotions in those green eyes, wondering what pulled at the girl's heart so.

"You are concerned about something?" Tima asked.

"Not really concerned." Sarah looked at Tima and grinned like she'd been caught in a lie. "I guess concerned is an accurate enough term. Dev...Redhawk said that you're a sort of medicine woman, is that right?"

"No, not medicine woman. They are very powerful and undergo special training. I have some skills as a healer."

"I'm sorry. I didn't know there was a difference."

"Healers treat many ailments with herbs and some physical skills. Keeho, our clan's medicine man, concentrates on the world outside the physical. His healing is done with prayers and special knowledge of the spirits. A medicine woman is very rare. She is part healer, part medicine man. The spirits choose women at birth to become medicine women, blessing them with spiritual talents that go beyond the physical realm we live in."

"I had no idea. But Redhawk told me that you see things in dreams...that you know what dreams mean."

"I have some skill with such visions. Why don't you tell me about these dreams of yours?"

"How do you know about my dreams?" Sarah asked nervously.

"You and I sleep in the same *chuka*."

"Oh, yeah." Sarah chuckled at her own forgetfulness. "I-I don't like dreaming. I sort of try not to anymore."

"You have seen bad things in the past?"

Sarah smiled but didn't answer.

"I understand," Tima answered the unspoken question.

"I have been having an unusual dream for some time

now…the same dream, in fact. It's not an altogether unpleasant dream, but I…well, I can't seem to get it out of my head. Is there any way to actually stop a dream? You know, stop it from happening?" Sarah unconsciously fingered the stone necklace around her neck.

"If you understand the nature of dreams, it is possible to have some control over your visions."

"And the nature of dreams would be?"

"It is important to know what dreams are. They're the spirits' way of communicating with us. They share with us in this manner, but we do not always understand their language. They do not think as humans do, therefore, we find their messages confusing."

"What about people who don't believe in your spirits? Even they have dreams."

Tima smiled in understanding. "Very true, but just because they do not believe in the spirits does not mean the spirits do not believe in them."

Sarah enjoyed hearing Tima's logic. She decided to put her trust in the older woman. "I…well, I got this necklace and ever since I put it on…that's when the dreams started." She looked over at Tima, shaking her head. "God, that was as clear as Mississippi mud, wasn't it?"

Tima chuckled along with Sarah. "Why don't you start your tale at the beginning instead of the middle? I think it will be clearer to me then."

Sarah told Tima of the necklace and how Devlin had told her about the legend of the *okchako-talia* stone. "Ever since I put it on, it's come true, the idea of dreaming about my heart's desire."

"And you find this something bad?"

"I suppose it wouldn't be bad if…if I understood my own feelings better. If I really knew what my heart's desire was." Sarah drew her knees up to her chest and held her head in her hands. "I'm so confused about what I want, even if I could get it."

"You worry over that which you cannot control, Little Salmon," Tima said, laying a hand on Sarah's back. "If these dreams truly do represent you heart's desire, perhaps they show you a reality that you simply don't know of yet."

"But what if I get my hopes up by what I dream, then it doesn't happen?"

"That is not possible."

"At all?" Sarah looked up, her expression brightening.

"Not at all."

"Oh," Sarah said in a soft voice. She looked out onto the prairie once again, her thoughts far away. "Oh, my," she said, thinking of the many implications that arose due to her newfound knowledge.

Sarah shivered slightly, the cold night air chillier than she had anticipated. She was so tired, but she didn't want to miss the dancers. Tima said that when the young people danced that night, their dance would tell a story. Sarah had no intention of missing it.

Sarah and Devlin sat on one side of *Miko* Kontonalah and his wife, Artamicha. Tima sat with one of her unmarried sisters to the *Miko's* left. Sarah chatted easily with Kontonalah, finding his dry sense of humor refreshing, but there were times when she didn't know if he was serious or teasing her. She would look at Devlin and Devlin would shake her head and smile, admitting that her grandfather loved flirting with pretty women almost as much as he enjoyed a good story.

Devlin caught sight of the small movement as another shiver ran through Sarah's body.

"Hey, you're not trying to get a fever, are you?" Devlin asked.

Sarah ran her hands up and down her arms. "No, just a little chillier than I thought out here. I think I got spoiled from the last few days of warm weather."

Devlin jumped up from the ground. "I'll be right back."

True to her word, Devlin returned in a matter of minutes.

"Here, this should help." She wrapped a rabbit and fox robe around Sarah's shoulders.

"Thank you." Sarah couldn't choke back the yawn that followed. "I swear, it's not the company," she added, followed by a wry smile.

"You should probably be asleep by now. I don't think you realize how sick you really were."

"Mm-hmm," Sarah replied. "But I don't want to miss the dancers."

Devlin smiled at the stubborn woman. Her heart took over and she didn't care how it looked to anyone.

"Then come here. I have a solution." Devlin urged Sarah to sit in front of her, pulling Sarah toward her until Sarah's back leaned against Devlin's chest. "This way, if you fall asleep, no one will know," she whispered.

Sarah felt Devlin's warm breath against her ear, unable to stop the shiver of desire that ran through her body from the moist kiss of air.

"Are you still cold?" Devlin ran her hand along the side of Sarah's arm.

Sarah hardly dared to speak, she was certain her voice would betray the need she felt. "No," she whispered.

Sarah turned to face Devlin. She had to see Devlin's face. The two women gazed at each other until Sarah's hand reached up to brush a stray lock of hair from across Devlin's eye.

God, how I love those eyes. Please, Dev, kiss me. Right here, right now.

The powerful magnetism of those blue eyes mesmerized Sarah. Finally, after what seemed like an eternity, Sarah thought that Devlin was somehow looking deep into her heart, seeing all that Sarah felt. Devlin leaned her face closer to Sarah's.

Devlin, in the meantime, felt herself just as trapped within the green eyes gazing up at her. When Sarah's hand brushed across Devlin's cheek, she thought she would melt from the intensity of the sensation. After what felt like a lifetime of staring into Sarah's unwavering gaze, Devlin thought she saw her own reflection, followed by a hint of passion in the green eyes. Her heart knew the action she would follow before her brain had time to register the need. All Devlin knew was that she had to kiss Sarah. Leaning her head toward Sarah's, Devlin came so close she could feel Sarah's sweet breath on her face.

"Little Salmon, can I get you some warm berry tea?"

Little Dove knelt expectantly before them. Sarah felt a frustrated growl come from Devlin's chest.

"Little Dove," Devlin said firmly. "You and I need to talk."

Devlin had watched for days as Little Dove followed Sarah around, waiting for an opportunity to pounce. She dismissed it as harmless, but this had been the final straw. Devlin excused herself from the warmth of Sarah's body, dragging the kneeling girl off to one side.

Sarah never moved, still thinking about what had almost happened. She wondered if it was real or if it had all been in her head. Had Devlin actually been jealous of the attention Little Dove had shown her? She desperately wished Devlin had simply kissed her so she would know where she stood.

Devlin returned and sat by Sarah's side. Little Dove sat with some girls her own age. Devlin didn't seem as though she wanted to share what the two had talked about, and Sarah was too nervous to ask.

Devlin sat by Sarah in silence for what seemed like an extraordinarily long moment. She thought for certain that Sarah was very receptive to the idea of sharing a kiss. Devlin could scarcely believe it. *This is it, snap out of it. At least do something innocent enough that you can laugh it off if it turns out she slaps your face.* Devlin sighed deeply and placed an arm around Sarah's shoulder.

When Devlin said, "Come back over here," Sarah knew that there was no place she would rather be.

Instead of just providing a shoulder for Sarah to lean on, Devlin sat with her legs crossed and pulled Sarah into her lap. Wrapping the fur tightly around Sarah, Devlin enjoyed the feel of Sarah's back against her chest.

Devlin's left hand rested on her knee until Sarah took a deep breath and boldly placed her hand atop Devlin's, entwining her small fingers within the grasp of the larger, slender fingers. Sarah lifted Devlin's hand and positioned it around her own waist, still not releasing her grip.

Devlin sat there in shock at Sarah's seemingly fearless move. Quite suddenly, the heat emanating from both women became fierce. When Sarah leaned back against Devlin's chest, hair brushing against Devlin's cheek, she prayed that Sarah's actions weren't simply a display of friendship. For Devlin, it was the moment. There would be no turning back once she expressed how she felt. Whether Sarah accepted it or not, it would change things, a great number of things.

Turning her face into the sweet smell of Sarah's hair, Devlin ran her right hand up Sarah's arm, gently squeezing her shoulder. She leaned in and merely meant to brush her cheek across the soft skin of Sarah's face, but Devlin's body unconsciously demanded more. Devlin leaned in and placed a feather-light kiss on Sarah's ear. She waited a brief moment, her heart in her throat, waiting for any hint of revulsion from Sarah, now held tightly in Devlin's arms. When none came, she moved her caress to Sarah's neck.

Devlin's kiss had been so tender and easy that it felt like the beat of a butterfly's wings against Sarah's skin. Before she thought about what she was doing, her eyes closed and her grip on Devlin's hand tightened. Then she tilted her head to one side ever so slightly until she felt the earnest press of Devlin's lips on her neck.

Stopping was the last thing on Devlin's mind, especially after Sarah's encouraging body language, but she knew that if she didn't slow down, she'd be throwing the beauty over her shoulder and carrying her off to a more secluded spot. That wasn't the way she wanted it to be with Sarah, not what she wanted for their first time together. Besides, a kiss and an embrace in the dark was one thing. Commitment to someone like her was another.

Devlin let her mouth travel up to Sarah's soft hair, placing a kiss there. Much to Devlin's delight, she thought she heard a small whimper of protest from Sarah when her lips stilled their kisses. Devlin wrapped her arms around Sarah's waist, trying to get her breathing under control.

Sarah enjoyed Devlin's kisses much more than she thought she ought to be. Her mind was a million miles away until it drew her attention to a throbbing ache that began to develop farther south. When Devlin stopped and wrapped strong arms around Sarah, she thought she must be in heaven. She leaned back against Devlin and felt Devlin's heartbeat against her back, the rhythm as erratic as her own.

"You okay?" Devlin whispered in her ear.

"Oh, yeah," Sarah said, her voice cracking. She felt Devlin's smile against her ear. "You?"

"Oh, yeah," Devlin repeated. Her voice purred the response.

The dancers came on a few moments later, but by that point, the two women were lost to their own private fantasies. Just as Devlin suspected, Sarah had fallen asleep by the end of the dancers' story. She slept even as the talking and socializing of the evening went on, safe in Devlin's warm and loving embrace.

"Sarah," Devlin whispered.

Sarah heard Devlin's voice from somewhere in the warm cocoon of Devlin's arms but ignored the sound, snuggling deeper into her chest.

"Sarah," Devlin whispered again, this time drawing the woman's name out in a hot breath close to Sarah's ear.

Sarah opened her eyes, instantly alert. Devlin helped the embarrassed woman to her feet, and they walked away from the center of the village toward Tima's *chuka* in silence, Devlin reached out and brushed her fingers against Sarah's. Feeling her hand wrapped within Devlin's gentle grasp, once again

Sarah was in awe at the tenderness. Devlin's body was all hard muscle but covered with soft female skin that had the feel of silk. When Devlin had kissed Sarah's neck earlier, Sarah had been amazed at how gentle the caresses were. A woman who could be as hard and unforgiving as the land around them, a woman who could kill a man with her bare hands had a touch as delicate and light as the first breeze of spring.

The two women stopped in front of the entrance to Tima's lodging, uncertain as to where they should go from there. Devlin knew there would be no nights spent together from that point on. Not until they could talk and not before Sarah was sure about what she was getting herself into. Devlin wanted Sarah but not simply for a night, not to satisfy a need for physical pleasure alone.

Devlin could scarcely believe it was her own brain generating such thoughts; they were ideas and feelings she hadn't felt for anyone before. She wanted Sarah in her life, as well as in her heart, and not for a day or even a year, but for the rest of their lives. But there was still the fear that she couldn't be what Sarah wanted or needed.

Even as Devlin processed her thoughts and feelings, Sarah's own heart and mind mirrored them, as she looked up lovingly into Devlin's clear blue eyes.

"I think maybe…maybe I should find another place to sleep," Devlin said in a halting tone. *How do I tell her that lying next to her would be too much of a temptation? God, I hope she understands.*

"I think…" Sarah looked at the ground, then up at Devlin once again. "…that might not be an altogether bad idea." *How do I tell her that sleeping next to her now would be agony? God, I hope she understands.*

They stood that way, neither wanting to turn away, afraid the delicate spell of the evening would be broken.

"Here," Sarah said. Standing on her tiptoes, she took the rabbit skin robe from her shoulders and placed it around Devlin's. "If I know you, you'll curl up into a ball somewhere

159

without building a fire and be sick as a dog by morning."

Devlin smiled, enjoying the idea of someone worrying about her in such a way. She reached around the slim waist, and pulled Sarah to her. Devlin hadn't prepared herself for the pure jolt of desire that swept through her when Sarah's body pressed against her own. She realized that if she didn't leave, they would be in serious trouble.

"You better get in there by the fire. I don't want you getting sick again." Devlin brushed her lips against Sarah's forehead, turned her around, and pushed her gently through the entrance flap. Both women emitted nearly silent groans of frustration.

Sarah smiled to herself, standing alone in the middle of the large tent. *Well, at least we're headed in the right direction. We pretty much settled the "are you interested in me" question.*

"Kind of…" Sarah said aloud, knitting her brows together, realizing the pair had actually said very little to each other. In Sarah's mind, it was as if she and Devlin had talked all evening, but in reality, they didn't settle anything. *Oh, God…this is going to be a long night!*

Devlin walked until she left the village, heading farther into the woods. Building a small fire, she lay on the cold ground and wrapped the rabbit skin robe around her.

Sarah's scent still clung to the fur, and she breathed it in deeply, the fragrance making her dizzy. Absorbing the warmth of the fire, Devlin let her mind's eye fill with a vision of Sarah, letting her hand drift slowly between her legs. Her eyes closed, and she imagined the way she would love Sarah, her breaths getting shorter, and her legs parting wider. Finally, imagining it was Sarah's hand stroking her slick folds, she climaxed with a ragged moan. *Oh, God, this is going to be a long night!*

Chapter Twelve

It was two days later when Sarah and Devlin said their goodbyes to friends and family of the clan. Sarah promised Tima they would bring the children for a visit soon, and Sarah made it clear to her new friends that they were always welcome at her ranch.

It was at least half a day's ride to the valley and the Double Deuce. Sarah and Devlin must have made an odd sight. They both wore their clan garb, the only clothes they had, riding bareback on Alto.

Sarah wasn't very experienced at riding bareback, so Devlin gave her a leg up and vaulted herself easily onto the horse's back behind Sarah. Of course, Devlin said it was to protect Sarah from falling, but with Devlin's strong arms situated around Sarah's waist, neither of them felt any need to complain.

They barely said a word to each other even with the better part of a day ahead of them. If only one of them had put voice to her musings, the other would have responded in kind, but as it was, each woman became lost to self-doubt.

Since Devlin hadn't brought up anything to do with their relationship, Sarah thought Devlin might have realized her mistake of the past week. In the meantime, Devlin figured that since Sarah hadn't said word one about what had transpired, Sarah must have thought twice and obviously wanted a way out. If two hearts breaking could have made a sound, the noise would have echoed off the hills.

The large cabin looked just the same. For some reason, Sarah thought it might look different. She felt as though she had certainly changed. It seemed a lifetime ago since the day she had taken off for her uncle's ranch. Hot tears hid just beneath the surface as she felt Devlin slip from behind her and dismount. Reaching up, Devlin helped Sarah from Alto's back.

Devlin couldn't control her actions as she allowed Sarah's body to slide against her own while helping Sarah from the saddle. Sarah surprised Devlin even more by not releasing her hold from around Devlin's neck and shoulders. Their eyes met and familiar stirrings of passion swept through them.

The look in Devlin's eye seemed to indicate that Sarah's previous thoughts might have been amiss.

"I-I thought, well, that maybe you didn't want this…want me," she finished softly, unable to meet Devlin's eyes.

"What?" Devlin asked in amazement. "But I thought you didn't…"

Devlin pulled Sarah to her in a fierce hug, shaking her head. "Oh, Sarah, not wanting you couldn't be further from the truth. We've got to work on this communication thing, huh?" she said teasingly.

Devlin pulled back to tenderly stroke Sarah's face, trying desperately to convey what was in her heart. When Sarah finally smiled, Devlin knew she had been successful. She leaned in closer to Sarah, about to experience Sarah's lips firsthand.

"Good, God!" Hank came around the corner. "I almost shot y'all." Hank had the barrel of a Greener shotgun leveled at the two women.

Before Hank came any closer, Devlin whispered in Sarah's ear. "Somehow, some way, sooner or later, I am going to kiss you, Sarah Tolliver."

The two women exchanged a frustrated grin as they turned to greet their friend.

They all had a meal together, Sarah filling Hank in on her accident and their time in the village. Of course, there were gaps in the story where Sarah had intentionally left out bits of information regarding her and Devlin, but Hank smiled politely.

Sarah wanted to see her children and the rest of her family as soon as possible. Devlin refused to let her go off on her own again, at least not when coming so close to losing Sarah was still fresh in her mind. Hank agreed to stay on at the Double Deuce for another couple of days so they wouldn't have to rush back.

Devlin saddled Alto with her spare saddle. She and Hank chatted amiably while waiting for Sarah.

"You sure you don't mind stayin' here, Hank?" Devlin asked, tightening the cinch on Alto's new saddle. The horse fidgeted at the familiar weight on her back.

"Nah, besides, I figured after the last time, there's no way you wouldn't go with her." Hank grinned. He had come upon the two women in an embrace and knew things must have changed between them. As to how far those changes went, he could only guess since Devlin was being rather closed-mouth about the subject.

Hank told Devlin about the strangers he had caught watching the ranch.

"Watching?"

"Yep. They weren't rustlin' cows, just hangin' out up on the ridge watchin' the place. That's why I had the Greener ready when I happened on you two."

"I sure don't like the sound of that. Smells like a setup to me."

"What for?"

Devlin shook her head. She didn't know why or who was being set up. It was always possible that somebody had an old score to settle with her. Devlin's belly clenched at the idea of dragging Sarah into a life like that, always worrying whether someone with a grudge would want to take her on.

She slipped the Winchester she had saved from Telemachus's saddle into the leather holster on the side of Alto's saddle. She carefully checked her pistols, noticing that their weight felt odd on her hips. During the time she spent with Sarah in the village, her guns had been tucked away in her saddlebags. It was the longest she'd been without them strapped to her body in nearly twelve years. Devlin had reason for her extra caution.

Sarah walked out of the cabin, dressed once again in riding garments. "I owe Matt some pants after my last jaunt."

Hank excused himself, saying he'd go and saddle up another pony for Sarah.

Sarah watched as Devlin ran her fingers through the long mane that was usually tucked under her hat. The flames had claimed Devlin's beloved Stetson when she had been forced to burn their belongings. Sarah had her own hat hanging down her back, the cord suspended loosely around her neck. In her hands, she held a soft brown Stetson that showed its age but looked well cared for.

"I know how hard these are to break in. I thought maybe you'd like to have this one," Sarah said tentatively.

Devlin looked at the hat Sarah held in her outstretched hands. She felt strange enough wearing some of the dead husband's clothes, but his hat. She stared at it, looking uncomfortable.

"It's not Peter's, Dev." Sarah said softly. "It belonged to my father."

Devlin looked into the green gaze that immediately made her knees weak. "Sarah…I…" Devlin was at a loss.

"It's okay if you don't want it." Sarah smiled, not wanting to push.

"It's not that, but it belonged to your father. Shouldn't it go to Matt or—"

"I think my father would have wanted someone like you to have it. I think he would have liked you."

Devlin reached out for the hat, pulling Sarah's hand toward her. With their bodies inches from each other, Devlin smiled and leaned down to whisper in Sarah's ear.

"I think you're giving your father way too much credit, 'cause if he knew what I was thinking half the time about his daughter, he'd have wanted to shoot me, not shake my hand."

Sarah felt the implication of the statement deep in her abdomen, then when Devlin followed it up with one of her sultry smiles, Sarah was nearly on her knees.

Hank came around the corner with a saddled Appaloosa, once again interrupting the two women in the middle of an embrace. Devlin quickly pulled away from Sarah, but not before taking note of the blush on Sarah's face. It was a little thing, but it was a great encouragement to Devlin.

"Your timing's perfect." Devlin growled at Hank.

"Hey, I gave ya ten minutes by my pocket watch. If you can't kiss a girl in ten minutes, you're doing it wrong!"

Sarah laughed aloud. This time, it was Devlin's turn to turn red.

They rode for a few hours before coming upon a herd pasturing in a green valley. They were both surprised by the wrangler on the ridge.

"Well, look what the cat dragged over my way," Art Winston said to the two women.

"Uncle Art, what are you doing riding herd?" Sarah asked as she and Devlin pulled their mounts up next to him.

"Well, I can't let the young pups have all the fun. Actually, I got everybody out on the prairie already, and one of the younger fellas came down with a bellyache and a fever. With Hank over at your place, that left only me."

"Sorry about that. Why don't you let me take over out here, Mr. Winston?" Devlin said.

"What and let you have all the fun?" He winked at Devlin. "I think I forgot what fresh air and exercise was."

Devlin smiled at him. They rode a small way together while Art chatted with his niece, who had become more of a daughter to him over the years. Sarah told him of the accident she had on Telemachus and how Devlin had rescued her. Sarah left out the part about how sick she became.

"Guess I had you pegged right from the start, Dev. Knew you were the only one that could keep up with her." He indicated Sarah with a jerk of his thumb.

Art didn't miss the look that passed between the two women. He noticed the hat Devlin wore right away, recognizing it as his brother's beloved Stetson. It didn't seem to faze Art much, but he'd been out in the wild country a long time. In fact, nothing much surprised him anymore. He thought it funny somehow. He'd learned that in the untamed country, all the old rules didn't apply anymore. Back in Kentucky, the boys would have hanged Devlin from the closest tree. In the territory, Art thought what a good match Devlin made for Sarah.

What happened next became a blur in Sarah's mind. One minute she listened to her uncle talk, the next moment his head jerked back, his body thrown from his saddle. It was almost as if the crack of the rifle came after, but Sarah knew it was the echo.

Devlin didn't even look around; her body reacted to the sound. She flew across her horse, hitting Sarah's shoulder and knocking them both to the ground. Devlin rolled and took the weight of Sarah's smaller body hitting her own, grunting when her back hit the dirt with a thud.

A looming cliff face shadowed over the pair as Devlin checked Sarah under her. "Sarah, are you okay?"

Sarah couldn't speak. She looked past Devlin to where her uncle lay. Devlin looked up into the sun, determining that the shooter was somewhere in the rocks they hid under. The shooter had only taken one shot and was moving to a new position to finish them off or had already gotten what he came for and fled. Either way, Devlin needed to know.

She moved away from Sarah, crawling on her belly under Alto's body. The horse had reared at the shot but stayed where her mistress could reach her. Devlin reached Art, placing her fingers against the pulse point at his neck. She looked back at Sarah, who watched intently, hoping for some sign of life from her uncle. Devlin shook her head.

Crawling back, Devlin wrapped Sarah in her arms, the smaller woman shaking with rage and tears.

"Sarah, I need to go up there and take a look." Devlin knew no other way to say it.

"No! Please, Dev, don't go."

"We're sitting ducks here. I have to. Please, honey, stay here."

Devlin let out a low whistle, and Alto came closer to the rocks. Standing up quickly, Devlin slipped the Winchester from its leather holster and handed it to Sarah.

"Point this like you mean to use it at anybody who gets here before me, even if you know them. Understand?"

Sarah nodded, and Devlin touched her cheek before climbing among the boulders and disappearing from view. It didn't take long for her to reappear.

"It's okay." She pulled Sarah up and held her in a strong embrace. "They're gone now. Couple of cigarettes up there, like they were waiting."

"Dev, who could have wanted to kill Uncle Art?" Sarah asked between sobs.

"I don't know, honey, but I'm damned well gonna find out," Devlin said as she held Sarah to her fiercely.

Devlin wrapped a blanket around Art's body and carefully placed him over the Appaloosa's back, tethering Art's mare to the pony.

"Please don't look back there," Devlin said.

She had Sarah ride in front of her on Alto. Sarah couldn't seem to stop crying, and Devlin wrapped one arm around her tightly; the other held Alto's reins. They must have made an odd-looking pair when they rode onto Winston land. Devlin relinquished Sarah to her older sister's care, immediately organizing a posse to search for the shooter. Devlin told them all she knew, which wasn't much. From the signs she saw, she recognized that there were two of them and they had headed into town.

The sun had already set by the time Devlin and the posse returned to the Winston ranch. Devlin took a few tentative steps into the huge main house, putting propriety aside to check on Sarah.

"Dev," Hannah squealed and jumped into Devlin's arms.

"Hey there, princess. Where's your mama?" Devlin asked, giving the girl a hearty hug.

"She's in bed. Want me to show ya where?"

"No, we better let her sleep. Besides, you should be in bed, too."

A stranger walked into the room from the kitchen, extending her hand to Devlin. "Go on, Devlin. Sarah told me to send you up when you got back. I'm Madeline Harrington, by the way."

Devlin shook hands with the woman. She must have been a good five years older than Sarah, taller, too, but spoke in the same lilting drawl. She had long auburn hair and the same green eyes, now red-rimmed. She'd obviously been crying.

"Sarah's already told me quite a bit about you. Did you find anything more out?" Madeline asked.

Devlin shook her head, wondering how much *quite a bit* was.

"Why don't you let Hannah show you upstairs? I know Sarah wants to know that you're all right. Then, young lady…" she pointed at Hannah, still in Devlin's arms. "I want you to go to sleep."

Devlin let Hannah down and followed the girl upstairs. Opening the door, she noticed Sarah was in bed and asleep, a haggard look on her still face.

"Shh," Devlin whispered, sitting in a chair at the foot of the bed and holding Hannah in her arms.

"Is Uncle Art dead, Dev?" Hannah asked.

The girl's question surprised Devlin. "Yes, princess."

"What's dead?" Hannah asked earnestly. "I asked Aunt Mattie and Matt, and nobody will tell me. Is it the same thing as die? 'Cause that's what happened to my daddy."

Devlin wasn't sure what she should tell the girl, but she was certain Sarah wouldn't want her to lie to Hannah. "Yes, sweetheart, they're the same thing."

"Does it mean you just go 'way?"

Devlin smiled and kissed the top of the girl's head. "Well, it's kind of like you've got a little pocket watch right in here." She placed the girl's hand on her own chest, covering it with her own. "Feel how it ticks along?" Hannah nodded. "Sometimes the little clock just stops ticking. It slows down or it gets broke. When the ticking stops, then you're dead, but it's not anything to be afraid of."

"Will it happen to you...and mama?"

"Someday, but I hope not for a long while yet."

"Then mama will be an angel!" Hannah said triumphantly.

Devlin let out a chuckle. "I think your mother is already an angel, don't you?"

The girl nodded and snuggled into Devlin's embrace. When Devlin looked up, she saw a pair of green eyes so filled with love it almost knocked her from her seat.

"Hi," Devlin said softly.

"Hi," Sarah repeated with a small smile.

Devlin deposited Hannah on the bed and walked over to a pitcher and bowl on the dressing table. She washed the trail grime from her face and hands, then knelt beside Sarah's bed, taking Sarah's hand in her own firm grasp.

"Are you crying 'cause Uncle Art is dead, Mama?" Hannah climbed into her mother's embrace.

"Yes, honey," Sarah said.

"But Dev says you shouldn't be afraid of being dead."

Sarah smiled at her daughter, then up at Devlin. "It's just that I'm going to miss him a lot, sweetheart."

Hannah seemed satisfied with the answer and snuggled under the blankets.

"You look tired," Sarah whispered. "Come here and lie down with us for a while." Sarah moved into the middle of the bed, pulling Hannah with her.

"I'm filthy from the trail," Devlin said.

"I don't care. I just want to feel you near me. Please, Dev," Sarah pleaded, tears filling her eyes.

Devlin had no intention of refusing Sarah anything, so she unlaced her moccasin boots and pulled them off. Removing her guns and laying them on the table, she lay on the soft bed on her side to face Sarah. Hannah squirmed slightly between the two women, while Devlin ran slender fingers through Sarah's blond locks, caressing Sarah's face.

"Mama, when we go back home, can Dev stay with us for always?" Hannah yawned sleepily.

Sarah and Devlin kept their eyes focused only on each other as Sarah answered the girl. "Is that what you'd like, honey, for Dev to stay with us always?" Sarah locked her gaze on the pair of blue eyes before her.

"Uh-huh." Hannah nodded while wearing a smile, then closed her eyes.

"Me too," Sarah admitted with a whisper. Sarah hoped the woman who lay next to her would understand her answer was for her, as well.

The corners of Devlin's mouth curled up at Sarah's response. It was the first verbal admission from Sarah confirming that she did indeed want a future with Devlin. Devlin felt too many emotions to speak. Sarah reached up and gently ran her fingertips across Devlin's lips. Devlin used her own hand to press the woman's fingers against her lips in a kiss, pulling Sarah's hand away slightly to place a gentle kiss in the palm of Sarah's hand.

As a declaration of love, it was an unexciting affair. Both women simply closed their eyes as sleep took them to another realm, the events of the day finally stealing over them.

Chapter Thirteen

"Sarah, what are you doing up so early?" Madeline asked. "Devlin told me you were rather sick after your accident."

"Mattie, you know me. I can't stand letting people take care of me."

"Oh, right," Madeline said sarcastically, walking toward the window that Sarah stood in front of, taking in the sight that her sister was fixed on.

Devlin stood casually with her hands on her hips, just above where her guns lay. She was speaking to a few men, obviously giving instructions on how to perform some task by the occasional gesturing of her arms. Devlin glared at the men she was talking to, but when she finished and the men walked away, she looked up into the window that granted her access to Sarah's image. Devlin's scowl was so quickly replaced by smiling blue eyes that Madeline swore she was looking at a different woman.

"Oh, right," Madeline repeated, letting the curtain fall back across the window. "Yeah, you're definitely not one to let anyone take care of you."

Sarah couldn't stop the blush or the look of satisfaction on her face.

"Does it bother you?" Sarah looked suddenly worried at her sister's reaction to her obvious affection for Devlin.

Madeline laughed. It was genuine, and after a day of so much sadness, it did both women's hearts good to hear it.

"Sarah, after living with you and father? Narrow-minded

is just not in me, especially when it comes to you." Madeline placed her arm across her sister's shoulder and pulled her closer. "It's about time you had a little happiness in your life. Besides, I talked with her this morning, and Devlin seems to care about you and the children a great deal. And I can see how taken with her Hannah and Matthew are." Madeline squeezed Sarah's shoulder. "It's time you forgive yourself. Not everything that happened when we were younger was your fault. Give yourself a break, okay?"

Sarah smiled. "Why weren't we this way with each other when we were younger?"

"We were both too busy being spoiled brats! I was too jealous of the way you got on with father, and you were too jealous of me and the time I had with mother."

"It's too bad we were such foolish girls," Sarah said. "We would have been unstoppable together."

Again, Mattie laughed. "Can you imagine? God, help Lexington if we had!"

Both women laughed and shared a hug before turning to the sound of a light rapping and the front door opening. Devlin walked inside and Sarah thought how much taller and stronger the woman looked when inside the confines of four walls as opposed to standing on the open prairie.

Devlin pulled off her hat and said good morning. "Hey, you should be taking it easy." Devlin touched Sarah's cheek in concern.

Sarah touched Devlin's hand and brought her own up to Devlin's face. Devlin glanced nervously at Mattie, who stood watching the pair.

Sarah pulled Devlin's chin until their eyes met. "It's okay."

Devlin realized Madeline held nothing but love on her face for Sarah.

Devlin smiled at Sarah and surprised both of them by brushing her lips softly against Sarah's forehead.

"You had kind of a rough day yesterday. I don't want you

out breaking ponies today."

"Yes, Devlin," Sarah said obediently.

"Devlin," Madeline called out as she held back the lace curtains to the window that faced the corral. "Do you know who that man is out there?"

Devlin still held Sarah's hand and the two women walked over to where Madeline stood. Madeline indicated a man in the midst of a half-dozen wranglers entering the corral. Devlin tried to search the men's faces, but most of them began dismounting and pulling saddles from their mounts, their actions hiding their features.

"I can't tell who you mean, why?" Devlin asked.

"There's a youngish man among them. He took sick yesterday, that's why Uncle Art rode herd. When I sent Chang out with some tea and broth for him, he said the man was gone. The trail boss, R.J., said that happens with young hands, they up and take off sometimes. I think it's odd that he's back now. There, there he is by the barn."

Devlin looked over to where Mattie pointed. Sarah felt Devlin's hand tighten around her own.

"Dev, do you know him?" Sarah whispered.

Devlin felt herself go numb at the sight of the younger wrangler. A memory flashed in her mind. The traitorous members of her gang held her down and pistol-whipped her after she had unsuccessfully tried to stop the rape of the girl from the ranch in Pawnee. The man who had hit Devlin the hardest and smiled the biggest stood chatting to the trail boss not fifty feet from her.

"Where are the children?" Devlin asked quickly.

"Upstairs, they're all still in bed," Mattie answered.

"Stay in here...both of you."

Sarah didn't argue. She felt the emotions flowing from Devlin's body in waves. She and her sister drew back from the window but only until they could still see the corral area.

Without her old boots and spurs, Devlin's feet hit the ground without a sound. The moccasins caused a mere whisper in the dirt. By the time Devlin stood behind the man Madeline had pointed out, R.J. was already speaking to her.

"Can you believe he rides out yesterday and wants a job again today?" he asked Devlin.

Devlin didn't wait for recognition to dawn in the man's face. Devlin Brown wouldn't have been a forgettable woman in any man's mind. The young wrangler could only pray that the woman towering over him wouldn't be able to place him. He was so wrong.

Devlin wrapped an iron grip around the mans throat, the young man moving a petrified hand toward his holster. She squeezed her fingers tighter until he gasped for breath.

"Whatchya goin' for here?" She grabbed his gun hand by the wrist before it touched the grip of his pistol. Rotating the wrist in her grip sharply, the man let out a sharp scream as the sound of his own bones snapping filled his ears. Devlin brought her knee up and drove it into the man's crotch, releasing her handhold around his throat as the man dropped, moaning, to the ground.

"All right, let's start at the beginning," Devlin drawled, grabbing the front of the young man's shirt and pulling him to his feet. The narrow gaze that burned blue fire and the feral smile that spread across her lips became a warning sign, as other wranglers backed up, so as not to become involved in the certain pain that was about to be inflicted.

"I'm gonna ask you this twice, seein' as I believe in givin' everybody a second chance. If I have to ask you a third time, I'm gonna blow your kneecaps apart, one at a time." Devlin pulled her pistol from its holster, cocking back the hammer in front of the trembling man's nose.

"Who hired you to set up the old man?"

When Sarah heard Devlin's question, she realized what Devlin suspected the young man had done.

"I can't hear you," Devlin said. His silence continued.

She sighed. "One more time." She paused to let the ultimatum sink in. "Who hired you to set up the old man?"

"If I tell you, they'll kill me." He groaned in pain.

"Well, if ya don't tell me, I'll kill ya, and guess who's got ya now?" Devlin sneered.

If the young man had any thoughts about the woman's humanity and whether there really would be a third opportunity, he squashed any chance he might have had by his next action. Rearing back his head, the man spit in Devlin's face.

She stopped all motion and wiped the spittle from her cheek with a gloved hand. When she raised her face to the young man, the smile on her lips unnerved him more than anything else she'd done to him so far. Lowering her right hand, she pulled the trigger without looking.

The man screamed in pain as the bullet ripped through his kneecap. His body crumpled in on itself and he laid in the dirt writhing in agony.

"Montgomery...Montgomery hired us," he cried out.

"That son of a bitch," Sarah screamed as she tore through the front door on her way to the corral.

Devlin turned when she heard Sarah's scream, realizing she had been watching the entire incident. Sarah ran straight for the nearest horse in the corral.

"Sarah!" Devlin shouted.

Devlin raced the overwrought woman down just as she was about to leap onto one of the already saddled ponies. Devlin had to grab her around the waist and lift her, kicking, clear off the ground to stop her.

"Sarah, stop!" She pulled the smaller woman's body tightly against her own, feeling Sarah's sobs convulse through her body.

"Think about what you're doing. If this is true, you'll be doing exactly what Montgomery wants you to do, going off half-cocked like this. Do you think if he was responsible for Art's death, he'll mind one bit about blowing some woman's pretty little head off?" Devlin's words began to have an effect on Sarah. It was her final say that had the most impact.

"What would happen to Hannah and Matt? What would

they do without you? What would I do without you?" Devlin's voice cracked slightly. "Let me take care of this. It's what I do best."

The click of a gun's hammer alerted Devlin. Turning, Devlin looked into the defeated face of the man she'd just shot. She also looked straight into the barrel of his six gun. He was still on one knee, but only twenty feet or so from where Devlin and Sarah stood. Devlin immediately positioned her body in front of Sarah's. The man pointed his gun at Devlin's chest, but his hand shook and he swayed from side to side.

"Did ya tell yer little girlfriend there how we fucked ya after we beat ya up?" A smug smile on the kneeling man's face indicated that he thought he'd gained the upper hand.

Devlin's eyes narrowed, taking in the sound of Sarah's small gasp, but her face remained impassive. Devlin merely watched the young man and the way he moved his body. She watched, waiting for the flaw to appear. It always did, if she was patient enough. That crease in time that allowed her to read the thoughts in a man's head before his brain could order the action taken.

The wind caught one side of the barn door and it slammed against its frame loudly. The young man was good. He never turned his head, but his eyes jerked toward the sound. Devlin felt it was all the chance she would get. She drew one gun with dazzling speed and fired three rounds, slamming the young man's body into the barn wall. His own shot hit into the reddish brown dirt, impotently ricocheting away from them.

Devlin scanned the men still standing around her, silently evaluating whether there were any others in the crowd who belonged to Montgomery. She twirled her gun once and flipped it back into her holster. It wasn't a showy move; it had merely become habit over the years. Her thoughts immediately went to Sarah. Turning, she realized Sarah had never seen her kill anyone. Devlin wondered how it would affect her.

"Are you okay?" Sarah put her hands on Devlin's waist.

"Yes," Devlin said. Without caring how it looked, she

wrapped her arms around Sarah and held her close.

"What he said Dev…is it true?"

Devlin replayed the dead man's words over again inside her head. *Had she remembered? How could she ever forget the men who violated her on that day?*

"Later…" she said, knowing she would tell Sarah the whole story but not until they could be alone.

A scream from inside the house drew their attention away.

"Sarah…Devlin!" Madeline shouted in near hysteria as the front door flew open with a bang.

Both women already moved in that direction, but when they saw Matt's bleeding face at the door, they took off at a run.

"My God, Matthew, what happened?" Sarah wrapped her arms around her sobbing son.

"I tried to stop 'em." The boy looked up at Devlin. "I tried."

Devlin ran a hand through the boy's hair. Matthew had a split lip and a narrow cut along his right cheek that looked worse than it was.

"They took Hannah," Madeline cried.

It was as if the world stopped for Sarah. The hands that had been caressing her son's head stilled. Suddenly, there was no air to be had in the space around her. She turned to Devlin.

"Dev?" she uttered in a small voice.

Devlin rushed up the stairs, taking them three at a time, her long strides eating up the distance between the first floor and the children's bedrooms. The room looked tossed about, the window remained open, and a tall ladder still rested against the outside of the large ranch house. A small knife held a piece of notepaper against the bedside table. Devlin pulled the knife out and read the words, even as she felt her own heart ripped in two.

"Dev?" Again Devlin's name was the only question from Sarah's lips.

Devlin handed the note to Sarah and held the small woman

as her tortured cries echoed throughout the house.

The flames from the fireplace became the only illumination in the small den that belonged to Art Winston. Devlin leaned back on the long leather couch, one foot on the floor, the other resting along the length of the couch. Between her legs, Sarah lay, wrapped in a wool blanket, her head resting against Devlin's chest. The grandfather clock chimed in the front parlor and Devlin squeezed her in a gentle hug.

"Sarah, it's almost time, honey. We need to get up."

Devlin eased her body up from the comfortable couch, finding it difficult to tear herself away from Sarah's warm embrace. The note that had been left in Hannah's room explained that Devlin and Sarah were to meet a messenger at the entrance to the Winston ranch at nine o'clock in the evening. The messenger would give them instructions regarding what they would have to do to have Hannah returned to them. As long as the messenger returned unharmed, Hannah would remain unhurt.

Standing at the gates indicating Winston property, Devlin heard the rider come in long before he arrived. She lit a lantern and held it up, directing Sarah to stand back in the shadows.

"Here's my calling card. They said you'd recognize it," the young man said.

Looking at the colorful material, Devlin recognized it as Hannah's frock.

"I sure hope that girl don't catch cold wearing nothing but her slip. That would make me very angry, and you don't want to see me angry." Devlin looked into the young man's eyes.

The man shifted uncomfortably in his saddle under Devlin's icy gaze. The deathly calm surrounding Devlin unnerved him. None of their gang had expected to come back from this particular chore, so they all threw dice. He had lost. He waited for Devlin to pull her guns and blow him to hell. He waited so intently in fact, that it took him a few moments before he realized Devlin impatiently waited for him to continue.

"Uh, yeah…um, this is for the woman."

Devlin reached her hand out. "I'll see she gets it."

"Nope." The man pulled his hand back. "She's supposed to take it from my hands."

Sarah stepped into the light and took the offered envelope. She opened it and scanned the documents, handing them to Devlin. Devlin held them up to the light. They were deeds, not only to Sarah's land, but also to Art Winston's. Montgomery assumed that Sarah would be Winston's beneficiary.

"Tell the bastard I hope he burns in hell," Sarah said vehemently.

Devlin had never heard such a vitriolic tone to Sarah's voice before. She recognized the look in Sarah's eye and the tone of her voice, reminding her of a wounded grizzly defending her cubs.

The young man tried to ignore Devlin. "You're to sign the papers and bring them to town at midmorning. Just you and Devlin," he addressed Sarah. "You exchange the papers for the girl and no one gets hurt. You and your family go back to wherever you came from. Any funny stuff…" He looked at Devlin. "And the girl dies. You do anything different from the way I just told you and the kid dies. Any questions?"

"No questions," Devlin said. She let the man turn and leave, listening to the sounds of his horse galloping away before she and Sarah walked back to the house.

Everyone else had gone to bed and Sarah encouraged Madeline to do the same. Devlin tried to persuade Sarah to go upstairs, explaining that there was little they could do until morning, but Sarah grabbed Devlin's hand and led her back to the den and the warm fire.

"Sit with me?" Sarah asked.

Devlin resumed her position on the leather couch, feeling only slightly better when she was once again holding Sarah in her arms. Devlin had spent the remainder of the day fighting off the self-loathing that had overcome her, cursing herself for the ineffectualness that had caused Hannah's kidnapping.

After a long stretch of silence, Sarah murmured against Devlin's neck. "Dev, can you talk about it, the day that man was talking about? Was he telling the truth?"

Devlin rested her chin on top of Sarah's head. She had tried to avoid revisiting the memories of that day. Occasionally, the images came to her in nightmares, which often left her shaken and unable to return to sleep, sitting alone in the dark and waiting for the sun to rise. It felt different now. Sarah had already helped Devlin to conquer some of those old demons by knocking down the walls around Devlin's heart.

Taking a deep breath, Devlin told Sarah in vivid detail about the events of that day. How she had been beaten, shot, raped repeatedly, then left for dead by the members of her gang, all because she had attempted to stop the same from occurring to a young woman whose parents the out-of-control men had murdered.

"Your own men?"

"You have to remember what kind of men they were in the first place, thieves and scoundrels most of them. Almost all of them had killed a man at one time or another. Violence had lost its impact for them a long time back."

"I would have thought they respected you as their leader at least."

"Dale Karsten, he was my second-in-command. He was just waiting for an opportunity. He wanted to overthrow me as the leader of the gang since the day we became partners." Devlin ended her tale without telling Sarah that she would always remember Karsten's face as the one who took her first.

By the time her story was finished, Devlin had tears streaming down her face. Sarah sat up and beckoned Devlin into her embrace. As Sarah's arms enclosed around the woman whose heart belonged to her, she felt Devlin's silent sobs shake her body with their intensity. It hadn't been the pain or humiliation, which Devlin had kept to herself over the years, that tore at her heart the most, but rather the betrayal of her own men, some of whom she had trusted with her life on more than one occasion.

"I'm sorry I couldn't protect Hannah. I can't promise you that something like this will never happen again. There are always going to be people from my past that are going to want to hurt the ones I love, just to get to me. That man I killed today, he was one of the men from my old gang. I'm afraid Montgomery has hired those men to help him with this land fight, to kill your uncle and kidnap Hannah."

Then Devlin said something so fully out of character that she scarcely believed they were her own lips speaking the words. "Sarah, please don't leave me."

Sarah understood the fear Devlin had of abandonment and betrayal a little better. Nearly, everyone Devlin ever loved left her or broke faith with her. Softly kissing Devlin on a cheek still damp with tears, Sarah reassured Devlin that she would love her no matter what the woman's past held or what darkness her future might bring to them. Sarah knew in her heart that she and Devlin were destined to be together. She had no idea how she knew such a thing, but somehow she did. Although their pasts might intervene occasionally and life might not always be easy for the two women, the headstrong young woman finally felt as if she truly found the dark warrior of her soul.

"Never, Dev. I'll never let you go," Sarah whispered.

Devlin's internal timepiece woke her sometime before dawn. The fire had burned down to coals, leaving the room in darkness. Even in the blackness, she could feel that Sarah was not beside her. Seeing a crack of light, she opened the door to Art Winston's private office.

"Don't do it, Sarah!" Devlin said.

Sarah sat at her uncle's desk, poised to place her signature on the deeds, signing over the land to John Montgomery. She looked up in surprise.

"If you do this, then he wins," Devlin said.

"Oh, Dev." Sarah's reddened eyes filled with tears again.

"He's already won. Who else should I wait for him to take from me? Matt, Mattie…you?"

"Sarah, honey..." Devlin bent to one knee in front of Sarah, looking into her eyes. "Do you think Montgomery's going to let us just ride away after you give him those papers?"

"But he said—"

"Do you think he can afford to leave you as a witness to what he's done? It won't matter if you're a thousand miles away, you'll still be a witness to his crimes. I know people like John Montgomery. In fact, I was him once, and people like that don't leave things undone. Sarah, do you trust me?"

Devlin waited until Sarah lifted her face and nodded before continuing. "Trust me with your life, with the lives of your children?"

"Absolutely," Sarah said without hesitation.

"Then I'm asking you to trust me now. Let's do this my way. I promise you, I'll die before I let anything happen to Hannah or you. Remember what you said to me that night, before you pulled that bullet out of me? Well, I don't want to lose you, either, but I need you to trust me now."

Sarah stared down into her lap at her hands for a few long minutes. Finally, she looked up into the gaze that swept her away with its intensity.

"I trust you," Sarah said at last. "Completely."

Chapter Fourteen

Devlin spoke with Hank just before she and Sarah were to leave for town. She slipped an object wrapped in a blanket under the seat of the wagon. The morning was overcast, and it felt like rain as thunderheads moved into the valley.

"I don't know how many there'll be, I'm guessing around twenty."

Hank stood next to his friend finalizing their plan. A half-dozen wranglers had been sent over to the Double Deuce to run herd and take care of the ranch. Hank returned as soon as word had reached him about Art Winston's murder. Devlin asked for volunteers, picking out a dozen men who she knew as loyal to Art and who she trusted.

"Remember, these boys are cowhands, Dev, not gunmen," Hank said.

"Hopefully, it won't come to anything like that. If it's Dale, he and I will end it right there. I'm betting if he goes down, the others will lose steam in a hurry. That's the way they are. Then it's just a matter of showing we got more firepower than them and tossing them out of town. Remember, they'll be too busy to watch the roads, but you'll have to be careful once you get near town. I'm sure Karsten knows I'm not gonna let him just waltz away, but Montgomery's stupid, and that makes him unpredictable. You'll have to sneak into town after Sarah and I get there. And another thing, make sure everybody understands that I'll kill the first man myself who starts anything before I have Hannah."

Devlin ran her fingers through her hair and replaced her

hat. She had a dull ache in the back of her head caused by tension. A gunfight would be different for her. She admitted to herself that some of her edge was gone, replaced with a need to live, a need to protect the people she cared about. When she was known as the fastest gun in the territory, she cared about no one, least of all herself. She was good for one reason—she didn't care whether she lived or died. Now she had a reason to care, and things like that made a gunfighter make mistakes.

"Other than me, Sarah is going to be the only one they'll allow to get close enough to Montgomery or Karsten." Devlin looked down at the object she'd placed under the wagon's seat. "Frankly, she's a better shot than you are." Devlin gave Hank a wry smile.

"One last thing. If I go down, I don't care what else happens. I want you to promise me that you'll get Sarah and Hannah out of there. I'll need you to get them all as far away from here as fast as you can."

Hank gripped his friend's hand tightly. "You can count on me, Dev."

Then both did something out of character. They shared a brief, but heartfelt embrace.

Sarah walked out of the house after kissing Matthew and Madeline. Devlin watched her, noting the previous day's look of defeat had been replaced with one of grim determination. Devlin had helped to put that expression there. She hoped that she hadn't filled Sarah with any false expectations.

Devlin told Sarah on the way to town the way she wanted the plan to transpire. Sarah was quiet, but she knew no amount of arguing could keep Devlin from doing this. Besides, she agreed to trust Devlin with her child's life, and she meant it. She also knew that Devlin had been right. Even if she did sign over the deeds, it wasn't likely that John Montgomery would let them walk away.

"I'm going to ask you to do something that I really never wanted to. I'm hoping it won't even become necessary," Devlin said.

"Anything, Dev, you know that." Sarah answered so quickly, with such strength of conviction, that Devlin had to look over at the woman in pure wonder. The unconditional love Sarah offered amazed Devlin.

"What one thing did I do right in my life to deserve you?" Devlin touched a gloved hand to Sarah's cheek.

Devlin's loving gaze would always be enough for Sarah. She prayed to every god of the white man and of the clan, asking only for the safety of her children and the woman she loved.

Devlin's hand returned to the wagon team's reins. A worried expression remained on her face. "Sarah, I know you don't want to think about it, but we need to plan for the eventuality that something might happen to me," Devlin said.

"I know," Sarah said sadly.

"If Karsten takes me down, they're not going to want to let you and Hannah out of there. They must know by now that you're...well, with me. I mean, they'll think you've been with me..."

"And they'll want to hurt us because of that," Sarah finished.

"I'm afraid of what they'll do to you," Devlin said, barely speaking above a whisper.

"So what should I do?" Sarah circled her hand around Devlin's arm.

"If Karsten is dead, there's not much chance Montgomery will have the jewels to order anybody around. Hopefully, by that time, Hank and the boys will have shown up. Feel what's under your seat."

Sarah reached under the wooden seat and felt a blanket wrapped around a long, heavy object. She recognized her Winchester immediately.

"If Karsten kills me, you'll need to buy yourself some time, then you and Hannah take off in the wagon. Hank should be there by then, but I can't depend on that. Besides, you'll be the only one close enough to..." Devlin couldn't bring herself to actually say it aloud, what she was asking Sarah to do.

"I'll have to kill Karsten myself if we're to get out of there alive," Sarah said slowly.

The look of pain that settled on Devlin's face nearly broke Sarah's heart. Sarah leaned her head against Devlin's shoulder. "We'll be okay," Sarah whispered, leaning over and kissing Devlin's cheek. "We'll be okay."

They rode along not speaking and each woman lost in her own thoughts. Finally, Sarah broke the silence.

"How did you know? When that man was going to shoot you yesterday, how did you know when to draw on him? Is that what makes you so good with a gun?"

"Patience is the biggest part of it," Devlin said as calmly as if Sarah had just asked her a mathematics question. "You have to let go of anything else that might be happening around you, only focusing on the person in front of you. If you're patient and you watch close enough, you'll see the flaw."

"The flaw?"

"It's hard to describe, but everyone does it in some way. They telegraph their intentions. It's like their body lets you know what they're going to do, even before their brain has let them in on it. Sometimes it's a twitch of a facial muscle or the tic of an eye. Sometimes it's not even as obvious as that. It can be just a look in a man's eye that's different from the other looks he's been giving you. And sometimes, well, sometimes it's just a matter of luck."

Devlin finished just as the town loomed before them. She pulled the wagon to a stop and reached over to squeeze Sarah's hand. Sarah returned the affection.

"Sarah, before we start this, there's something I want you to know."

"No!" Sarah covered Devlin's lips with her fingers. She knew what Devlin was going to say. Devlin was going to voice the words that they hadn't yet spoken. They hadn't told each other that they were in love, but Sarah knew that's what Devlin was about to say.

"Don't say it. I don't want you thinking you've said your piece and now you can be all noble and go and die on me. I'd rather it be your reason for coming back to me."

Devlin smiled at Sarah's logic. Thunder grumbled and roared in the distance. Heat lightning flashed from up in the hills, and the air turned heavy. Devlin gave the reins a sharp snap, and the horses carried them down the road and into the town.

As they rode in, Devlin looked around the streets of the usually bustling town, suspiciously empty. She searched for signs of Karsten and his men, even as she appeared not to be. Counting the number of shadows in the saloon, Devlin thanked the spirits. When men milled about a saloon just as their leader was about to enter into a showdown, it was a sure sign that once he was dead, they'd be hopelessly lost.

Devlin pulled the wagon in front of Montgomery's Cattleman's Association office just as the stranger the night before had instructed them. She jumped from the wagon and looked around before moving to the other side. She left the wooden wheel brake off, and instead of wrapping the reins around the hook on the wagon, she slid them toward Sarah before jumping from the wagon.

John Montgomery sauntered out of his office as if the whole situation was under his control. The man had no idea he would probably die if Devlin lived long enough to finish the job.

"I believe you have something for me." He looked up expectantly at Sarah, taking a step or two toward the woman in the wagon.

"Right here." Devlin waved the papers.

Montgomery's face fell. He had wanted to have Sarah admit defeat, show her subservience to him by handing him the papers. Devlin knew that kind of power game too well. She not only had the papers in her possession, but she made him walk to her to get them. Once Montgomery stood before Devlin, he looked up at Sarah.

"Too bad you have such a perverted appetite, Sarah. You and I would have made a good team." He leered openly at her.

"John Montgomery, if we were the last two people on Earth—well…" Sarah smiled sweetly. "We'd be the last two people on Earth."

Montgomery appeared as though his good humor had come to an end and reached for the papers. Devlin quickly pulled them out of his reach.

"First the girl," she said in a low voice.

Montgomery's smile went broad at that suggestion. Devlin understood what that meant, even if Sarah didn't. Montgomery's cocky attitude indicated that they weren't meant to leave town. He yelled down the street and the door to the café opened up. Karsten came out leading Hannah. The girl was crying but looked unharmed. When she saw Devlin, she tried to run to her, but Karsten stopped her. Devlin walked down the middle of the street, slowly taking in every detail. She stopped about twenty feet from the gunman.

"Long time." Karsten grinned.

"Not long enough."

Devlin lowered herself to one knee. "Hannah, come here," she said warmly, holding one arm out to the girl.

Karsten didn't try to stop her. Hannah took off at a run and leapt into strong arms that swept her up in a crushing embrace. Being in familiar arms started Hannah crying once again. Devlin kissed her and whispered in her ear, turning her back on Karsten.

There were few men in the world who she would feel safe pulling such a maneuver on, but Devlin knew that Karsten wanted to beat her. Shooting her in the back wouldn't suit his purpose, just like shooting her and beating her hadn't been enough a couple of years earlier. That's why he encouraged the men to rape her. That's why he was the first in line. He didn't just want to win; he wanted Devlin to see it coming and to humiliate her as much as possible in the process.

Devlin walked toward Sarah and Montgomery with Hannah

in her arms. Devlin stopped halfway there. If Sarah was going to have a chance at running, should Devlin lose, Montgomery needed to be farther away from the wagon.

"Sarah, move the wagon to the other side of the street," Devlin shouted and Sarah immediately complied, the wagon groaning as the wheels turned sharply.

"Wait! She doesn't leave until I get the papers," Montgomery yelled.

"Then come and get 'em." Devlin held the papers in the air.

Montgomery seemed torn, but he looked as though he wanted the land more than he wanted Sarah. He walked toward Devlin. Devlin placed Hannah on the ground and whispered to the girl. Hannah took off toward her mother as fast as her six-year-old legs could carry her. Sarah jumped from the wagon and hugged the girl tightly.

Montgomery didn't seem to like the idea that his collateral was getting away or the fact that he had to walk up to Devlin to get his deeds. He developed a more confident air when he remembered Dale Karsten watched his back.

What Montgomery didn't realize was that paid guns usually have their own agenda and play by their own rules. Karsten didn't give a damn what Montgomery's feud was with the woman or Devlin Brown. He only knew that he wanted to take Devlin down for one final time, and when he was done with that, he'd think about her little girlfriend.

As Montgomery drew a hand forward to reach for the papers, Devlin grabbed his wrist, pulling it up behind his back. With their faces inches away, Devlin opened the deed to show him the blank white paper inside.

"You bitch!" Montgomery cried out.

Devlin spun the man and pulled back her arm for one of the most satisfying, nose-breaking punches she'd thrown in a very long while. She then held the man up as she kneed him in the groin, sending his jewels into his throat. With little effort, she pushed him away from her and into the dirt. Then she turned to face Karsten. On her way around, she glanced briefly at Sarah holding Hannah; it was the last thought she could afford to spare the other half of her heart until the last bit of business was over.

Sarah watched as Devlin turned to face the gunman. Sarah heard a whisper and turned as Ellen quietly called to her from the front door of the brothel. Sarah looked back at Devlin, suddenly refusing to take a chance on losing her. She knew Devlin and Karsten were in a place where only they existed. If she could get set, no one would notice her and they certainly wouldn't be expecting it.

Sarah whispered softly to her daughter and pointed to Ellen. Hannah nodded, smiling at their old friend. When Sarah released her daughter, the girl ran for the open door. Ellen waited for Sarah to follow but watched as her friend carefully and silently slid a Winchester rifle from under the seat of the wagon.

From where Sarah stood, she could see over Devlin's left shoulder, directly into the face of the gunfighter. She waited and watched, just as silent as the two in the middle of the street. Looking indifferently into the man's face, imagining in her mind's eye what Devlin's face looked like, Sarah raised the rifle slowly, keeping it camouflaged behind the wagon. She suspected Devlin's face looked as impassive as ever, eyes narrowing so you could scarcely tell her irises were made up of two shades of blue.

Sarah watched as Karsten stared at Devlin, his eyes unblinking and a small bead of sweat trickling down from his temple. Sarah saw it. It was just as Devlin had described. She saw the thought in his eye.

By the time Karsten's brain ordered his hand to draw his weapon, Sarah had already opened her mouth to scream out a warning to Devlin. Devlin had a half step on both of them, reaching for both her guns.

The last sensation the gunman felt, aside from the pain, was a metallic dryness in his mouth, and in a fraction of a heartbeat, he knew it was fear he tasted, the fear of his own death. He had barely cleared his holster when Devlin's thumbs cocked back the hammers of each pistol. He watched in horror as the woman's eyes turned pale, losing their color. He realized too late that he looked into the face of death.

Sarah's body jerked at the deafening explosions from Devlin's guns. Devlin emptied her pistols into the man. Karsten hit his knees, ending up face down in the dirt without firing a shot.

Devlin slowly walked over to the man, who still attempted to breathe.

"You got faster," he gasped as blood trickled from one corner of his mouth.

"Nope, you got slower," Devlin said without feeling.

"I'll see you in hell, Devlin Brown." Dale Karsten's heart finally stopped beating.

"There's every possibility," she said without inflection.

Devlin turned at the sound behind her, her hand going to her holster. She silently cursed herself. In her rage, she broke the first rule of staying alive. She had emptied both guns.

Looking up, Devlin watched as John Montgomery aimed a Derringer at her head. "Hellfire! Thirty-five years I made it, only to get my brains blown out by a fancy dude with a little peashooter."

The unexpected crack made Devlin flinch. The expression on Montgomery's face was one of incomprehension. He looked at Devlin, then down at his shirt, a red stain spreading across his chest. When he fell to his knees, Devlin saw behind Montgomery. There in the middle of the dirt road, Sarah stood frozen, the Winchester still aimed at the wounded man.

Montgomery turned his head to see Sarah there, then looked back at Devlin. The Derringer finally fell from his grasp.

"I never thought she had it in her," he mused.

"That was your second mistake," Devlin answered.

"Second? What was my first mistake?" he asked, dropping from his knees to fall flat on his face in the dirt.

Devlin leaned over the man and whispered, "Fucking with her in the first place!"

Like all the other men Devlin had used the line on, the sarcasm was lost on them. They were always too dead to care. The thunder rumbled and the lightning flickered from a long way off. Devlin crossed the street to stand beside Sarah.

"Sarah?" Devlin said gently.

Sarah lowered the rifle, but she still stared at the body of the man she had just killed. "I had to. Right?"

"Yes, honey. It was either him or me." Devlin pulled the gun from Sarah's grasp and placed her arm around Sarah.

Devlin pulled Sarah away from the carnage before them, walking down the street.

"Where's Hannah?" Devlin asked.

"She's okay. She's with Ellen. You were right, Dev. It does change everything."

"I'm sorry, baby." Devlin placed the rifle in the wagon but continued walking with her arm around Sarah. By the time Hank rode in, the two women had nearly walked to the edge of town. Sarah had finally become herself again, her mind eventually purging itself of the images of Montgomery's dead body.

"Timing, Hank, we got to work on that timing of yours." Devlin smiled up at her friend. "I think you'll find most of them in the saloon. Why don't you encourage them to move on?"

They were finally alone, and Devlin wrapped both arms tightly around Sarah. Pulling back slightly, the two women looked at each other.

"Sarah," Devlin began, both hands holding Sarah's face. "Do you know...do you have any idea what you mean to me?"

Sarah looked away as tears threatened. "Dev, I was...I thought I'd never meet someone like you. I feel as if I've been waiting for you to come into my life for so long. I've been so lonely waiting for you to come along."

"I know," Devlin whispered. "The tumbleweed notes."

"What?" Sarah hung her head, uncertain whether to be elated or humiliated.

"You wrote about your heart and tied them to tumbleweeds, didn't you?"

Sarah's face grew hot thinking Devlin had found the notes she had thrown to the wind. "It's just that I wanted so much from a lover. All my dreams told me that my warrior would come for me someday, but it got so hard to wait. Every day that went by made my heart ache a little more. I thought if I could just tie my heart to a tumbleweed, surely my warrior would be able to find it."

Devlin smiled at the woman who held her heart. Then she wrapped her arms around the smaller woman.

"She did, *sachu-kash*. She did."

Sarah couldn't speak. Devlin had used the language of the clan and called Sarah *my heart*. The intensity of her own emotions nearly swept her away.

The thunder rumbled low and long, and Sarah felt the vibration of it deep within her chest. Then the rain began to fall. The air was humid and still as the tiny droplets of precipitation fell onto their skin, soaking into their clothing. Time slowed for the two women as they let themselves go to the incredible sensations of their bodies held together by some unseen force.

Devlin pulled the soft brown hat off her head, the raven mane cascading onto her shoulders and down her back. She leaned her head back and closed her eyes, almost sensually, to the raindrops. Her arm around Sarah's shoulder held her body tightly to her own.

For the first time in her life, Devlin felt at peace, as if she was about to do something that had been fated for her all along. It felt so right. Being there felt so right. Sarah felt so right. Devlin felt as if her body had waited a thousand years for this one kiss, one perfect kiss to complete her, to heal the lonely ache in her soul.

Sarah felt as if her whole world had exploded into a million minuscule pieces and were rearranging themselves, gently falling into place again. The feelings of hopelessness and longing disappeared, replaced by a swirl of emotions that told her she was supposed to be there—there in Devlin's strong and loving embrace, the other half of her soul. The dark warrior Sarah's heart had waited on for centuries. She tightened her arms around Devlin's waist.

Devlin looked down into Sarah's emerald eyes as she felt the woman's hands press into the small of her back, pulling her closer. Devlin let her eyes close, suppressing a moan at the pleasurable sensation of Sarah's body against her own.

Once again, Devlin opened her eyes to look into the face of the angel who held her heart. Neither woman took any notice of the outside world around them. They held each other tightly as their gazes locked. Devlin reached one hand up to tenderly stroke Sarah's cheek with the back of her fingers. "So beautiful," she whispered.

Sarah turned her face and softly kissed the fingers that lingered on her cheek, tasting the saltiness of Devlin's skin, and mesmerized by the gentleness of the strong woman's touch. Sarah felt tears of joy fill her eyes, not knowing whether they spilled from her eyes or if it was the rain that ran in tiny drops down her cheeks.

Sarah slid her hands against Devlin's soaked back under her vest. Feeling the heat of Devlin's skin through her shirt, Sarah grabbed a handful of the cloth in each hand, and her body trembled at the powerful response her action had on Devlin.

Devlin felt Sarah's hands slip under her vest and the muscles in her lower belly clenched at the innocent intimacy. She wrapped her arms around Sarah, one hand reaching out to slip around Sarah's neck, fingers entwining in soft honey-colored locks. She slowly pulled Sarah's face closer.

The great spirit had been kind in stilling time for the two women. Mere moments had passed in the outside world around them, but for the two lovers, the instant could not be interrupted by the hands of time. They gazed at each other, conveying all that they held in their hearts, through their eyes.

Finally, Devlin leaned in to complete her destiny. Before their lips touched, she felt the warm breath of a sigh escape Sarah's lips. She felt the sweetness before their tongues intertwined. Savoring every precious heartbeat of anticipation, Devlin leaned in closer.

Sarah held her breath as Devlin's fingers tenderly tilted her chin upward. The penetrating blue gaze burned into Sarah's soul, searching the depths of her heart and branding her forever. Before their lips touched, Sarah knew that the dark warrior owned her body and soul.

As Devlin leaned down, Sarah raised herself slightly until each woman had breached the distance between her heart's desire. As their lips pressed together, ever so gently, each woman knew that this was the culmination of something extraordinary.

To Devlin, time no longer slowed, it had stopped altogether. She felt the soft, sensual lips of her love on her own, and when Devlin felt that the moment was as near to perfection as anything she had ever known, Devlin felt Sarah respond to the kiss. Silken lips moved against Devlin's own. She was no stranger to the pleasures of a woman, but Devlin had never tasted anything as sweet and wonderful as the mouth that now captured hers. Devlin's body entirely forfeited itself to the physical pleasure of the moment. She felt a delicious pressure on her back as Sarah slid her hands higher, urging her closer.

The tip of Devlin's tongue pressed itself lightly against Sarah's bottom lip, desiring a more intimate contact. Sarah's lips quickly parted to allow Devlin's tongue entry.

The taste of Devlin filled her mouth and Sarah almost swooned at the pleasure of it. She moaned into Devlin's mouth and the gentle kiss turned passionate, their tongues accepting, then giving pleasure to each other.

Devlin wrapped her hands within the amber locks. Moving

her feet apart to steady her stance, she pressed against Sarah's mouth. When Sarah moaned her pleasure into the kiss, Devlin felt a rush of liquid fire between her legs. She pulled away so they could take a much-needed breath, then she took Sarah's mouth again, a low growl captured within Sarah's kiss.

Sarah felt the low rumble deep inside Devlin's chest. It wasn't the growl of intimidation Devlin had used at Ellen's. The sound Sarah heard now was a growl of pure unadulterated lust and passion. It fluttered out from Devlin's chest, and Sarah felt it against her breasts, the vibration causing a tingling sensation against her skin.

Devlin pulled back and held Sarah's face in her calloused hands, moving her kisses over Sarah's cheeks and along her jawline, until she reached Sarah's ear.

"I love you, Sarah," Devlin whispered softly.

Pulling back to look into her lover's eyes, Devlin brushed the tears and the raindrops from Sarah's cheeks, her own tears mixing with the moisture from the sky and streaming down her tanned face.

"Oh, Dev, I feel like I've waited a lifetime to hear you say those words," Sarah whispered back. "I do love you, Devlin Brown. With all that I am, I love you."

Strong arms wrapped around Sarah's body as she nuzzled Devlin's wet neck. Devlin kissed the top of Sarah's head and held her close. Unwilling to end their embrace, the two women stood in the middle of the dirt road as the thunder continued its low rumblings. The rain, dropping steadily from the sky, fell unheeded around them.

Devlin had divulged the secrets of her wild warrior's heart into that one kiss, a wild heart tamed solely by the love and compassion of a small slip of a girl with a pride and bearing no queen could compare to.

In the end, it wasn't a gun that brought the fierce wrangler down, but rather a pair of green eyes and a stubborn heart as strong as Devlin's own.

You may also enjoy these Intaglio titles.

The Western Chronicles
by B. L. Miller & Vada Foster
ISBN: 1-933113-38-3
Price: $18.99

At the center of this story are two women; one a deadly gunslinger bitter from the injustices of her past, the other a gentle dreamer trying to escape the horrors of the present. Their destinies come together one fateful afternoon when the feared outlaw makes the choice to rescue a young woman in trouble. For her part, Josie Hunter considers the brief encounter at an end once the girl is safe, but Rebecca Cameron has other ideas....

The War Between The Hearts
by Nann Dunne
ISBN: 1-933113-27-8
Price: $16.95

Intent on serving the Union Army as a spy, Sarah-Bren Coulter disguises herself as a man and becomes a courier-scout for the Confederate Army. Soon the savagery of war shakes her to the core. She stifles her emotions so she can bear the guilt of sending men, and sometimes boys, into paths of destruction.

When Sarah is wounded and in danger of dying, her life is saved by a woman who stirs desire in Sarah for the first time. But Faith Pruitt is Sarah's enemy and betrays her into a hell worse than Sarah has ever known. Sometimes hearts are killed instead of bodies.

Can Faith save Sarah's heart and awaken her to love? Do they even want to try? Or are the women destined to be at war with each other forever?

Coming in June 2009

Prairie Fire
By LJ Maas
ISBN: 978-1-933113-47-0
Price $16.95

In this sequel to Tumbleweed Fever, the story of Devlin Brown, an ex-outlaw, and Sarah Tolliver, the woman of her heart, continues.

Sarah and Dev must convince the ranchers around them to destroy the wire fences that contain their cattle to avoid certain calamity. Amidst the beautiful and sometimes unforgiving land of the Oklahoma Territory, Sarah and Devlin begin a new life. Adventure and mysticism abound as they revisit the Choctaw camp.

Sarah must decide whether she will undergo the clan rituals that will allow her to join with the former outlaw in a ceremony that will bind their hearts together forever. Each woman must undergo an incredible test of her individual skills and all the while race against time to prevent a premonition from becoming a frightening reality.